D1534585

SCRATCHING THE HEAD OF
CHAIRMAN MAO

SCRATCHIN

OF CHAIRM

THE HEAD

MAO

JONATHAN TEL

TURTLE POINT PRESS *Brooklyn, New York*

Requests for permission to make copies of any part of the work should be sent to: Turtle Point Press, 208 Java Street, Fifth Floor, Brooklyn, NY 11222 info@turtlepointpress.com

Library of Congress Cataloging-in-Publication Data

Names: Tel, Jonathan. author.
Title: Scratching the head of chairman Mao / by Jonathan Tel.
Description: Brooklyn, NY : Turtle Point Press, 2019
Identifiers: LCCN 2019013851 (print) | LCCN 2019015659 (ebook)
ISBN 9781885983770 (ebook) | ISBN 9781885983725 (pbk. : alk. paper)
Subjects: | GSAFD: Suspense fiction.
Classification: LCC PS3620.E44 (ebook) | LCC PS3620.E44 S29 2019 (print)
DDC 813/.6—dc23
LC record available at https://lccn.loc.gov/2019013851

Design by Alban Fischer Design

Paperback ISBN: 978-1-885983-72-5
Ebook ISBN: 978-1-885983-77-0

Printed in the United States of America

This book was made possible with the financial assistance of the Qin Family Foundation. The foundation was established to honor the memory of Dr. Qin, whose untimely death deprived the world of a leading entrepreneur and philanthropist.

"Let all histories other than this one be burned."
—Emperor Qin Shihuang

CONTENTS

THE SHOE KING OF SHANGHAI

High columns and gleam and the drapes paper-white, the color of mourning, and murmured conversations and sweat and several varieties of important people, whose definitions he can only guess at, who are mostly dressed in black, negative spaces marking off the histories and levels and types of white, and the absence of tears, the absence of wailing, nobody who seems to be a relative or close friend, midday outside but inside a late afternoon, the light confused and hazy, everyone's breath rising and gathering in the high-ceilinged hall, *This place is a city of its own* (the same thought he had a month ago when he stumbled out of the train and there he was at last in Beijing West station), a condensed city, yes, large enough and small enough to generate a smog of its own, and meanwhile wreath-deliverers enter at intervals, trailing their lavish aromas, which mingle with incense and floor polish and an undersmell that might be rotten fruit and money as well as feet, for everyone is shoeless and so slightly abbreviated, celebrities in close-fitting suits are centimeters shorter than normal, a leading businessman is flanked by two bodyguards, dangerous and shuffling in their nylon socks, and he among them (he is the kind of man who is not looked at) painfully aware of his faded shirt and trousers and the hole in the left sock through which the smallest toe pokes, and he is trudging in flip-flops along the dried-up irrigation ditches of Sichuan, midsummer, white dust everywhere, the sheep trailing after, and from curls of conversation he gathers the man's name was Qin, he was a financier of some sort, at any rate he had financial links with those who have come to commemorate him, debits and credits, it was an overdose of sleeping pills, an accident, it is suggested, and nobody seems upset about this, there are small smiles when death is mentioned, along with *long time no see* and handshakes, for above a certain income level death is of less account, the rich maintaining their network of connections in Heaven and Hell, the dead puppeteer wriggling his fingers to make the mourners dance, whereas in Sichuan there is sorrow and music, the mourners screeching *How could you leave us just when things were starting to get better?* and here not only is there no particular sadness there is not even a body, who knows how death is done in Beijing, perhaps Qin is laid out deeper within the villa, perhaps that is where the true funeral is taking place (even financiers have relatives and people who love them), but he jumps back five minutes or so, the long brilliant dark cars double-parked like shoes along the drive, the chauffeurs smoking alongside, and clutching a wreath up against his chest as a shield he shuffles toward the marble stairs, the doorway, and by the shoe rack he nudges off his worn Flying Forward sneakers, and a servant relieves him of the wreath, taking it from his arms, exposing him, peeling off his disguise (yet he remains reasonably invisible), he steps onward and inward till he is back in himself, here and now, he takes one deep breath, holding the moment, and now he stays in this time but reverses space, and without ever having reached the vicinity of Qin, whoever that man might be, nor his ghost, nor the sly greedy god he will turn into, the migrant returns to the shoe rack and slides his socked feet into a pair of rather too large solid black brogues with a decoration of piercings in the upper and an obvious aura of expense, and, taller now, at least part of him wealthy, hardly limping at all, he strides out of the building and back down the drive past the sculpture of a turtle with a snake on its back and into the wreath shop van, now empty apart from a stray petal or leaf and fragrance, in due course he feels the bounce as an unseen driver gets in and a door slams and the engine starts up and he is delivered back to the heart of the city where he does not belong, but Beijing is full of people who do not belong so in a way he does.

He never intended to be a shoe thief. He moves backward and forward, into the past and into the future, retelling and revising his life in the capital, scribbling over it: he is hired at a construction site in Dongcheng (what is to be built is no concern of his, a skyscraper rising, story upon story), and he is a glazier, working with other glaziers, installing a pane and so on to the next pane, the west wind ceaseless above a given height, the entire site surrounded with a scenery wall depicting a joyous building, a concrete-and-glass festivity, and behold a high electronic billboard to count down the days and hours and minutes, the "death clock" they call it, or the "money clock" since when the clock subtracts to zero, the workers will be paid off and laid off, and the odd thing is how peasants recruited from his own village reappear on this site, look! there's old Bat Ears mixing cement, there's Crooked Nose in the kitchen tent, there's Worm Cast operating the controls of an earth-moving machine, here's himself eighteen floors up gripping a sheet of glass, his flock of sheep baahing in the horizonless urban smogscape; it's late morning and he's still up here, the wind pinned to his hair, the sun flying past, his fingers and shoulders concentrating on the job while his stomach dreams of lunch—steamed buns and egg-drop soup, with spicy Sichuan pickles— and he tastes it in anticipation, body and mind burping together, and he feels an odd rush past his face and torso, as if something is coming down from a higher level, though there is no higher level as yet, no workers on scaffolding perched above him, and there is a scream from below, another worker, a man he doesn't even know, hopping comically and shouting *aiya!*, and on the earth, next to the fallen man, clear as a diatom viewed through a microscope, a one-yuan coin—*his* coin, that must have escaped from his pocket, which it is true has a hole in it though surely too small, the coin must have zoomed from his hip like a UFO, and a foreshortened person down there brings over a bandage and winds it round and round the damaged leg-portion, and the victim gets up and more or less stands, and in dumb show the foreman sends him away, for what use is a cripple, however slightly crippled? and now the foreman's voice travels upward, "You, you're fired!" and he tries, "It wasn't me! It wasn't mine!" "You up there with the limp, come down!" *What* limp? —but even as he denies it, he feels it, not much more than a twisting in his left ankle, and with some difficulty he descends, and the man below who is led away looks from behind like himself, and he picks up the coin, its chrysanthemum design glowing on his palm, and the foreman tells him to go and not come back.

How can a man live in Beijing? He walks south, then west, he sees street performers, each wounded in his own way: a blind erhu player, a juggler with stick-out ears, a man who lies down on broken glass for a living, a conjuror who produces an orange from a woman's shoulder blade . . . briefly becoming all these freaks in turn, and then he follows the signs for the public toilet, and outside it an elderly water calligrapher is at work, master of a broomstick with a red sponge at its tip, dipping it into a pail and writing traditional four-character sayings on the paving: ANT DESTROY WHOLE DAM and LAMENT SMALLNESS GREAT OCEAN . . . couldn't he too write these, how tricky can it be, but if it were that easy everybody would be doing it already, the city would be full of calligraphers gripping sponge-tipped sticks and creating temporary characters on the sidewalks, every step you took you'd be walking on slippery wisdom, and with the unlucky coin he tips the calligrapher, who responds not in speech but in water, to the effect that a certain entrepreneur will pay for top-quality used shoes, no questions asked, and includes the address, also a sketch map, and the calligrapher gets back to his proverbs (the business advice is like a commercial between TV programs; the calligrapher must be paid for promoting the illegal shoe business, here, in this city of crooked motives) EVEN HARE BITE CORNERED and O FORTUNE O CALAMITY . . .

He limps west through Qianmen, earphoned citizens each accompanied by private music, to a restaurant street and a street of antiques dealers, and around the corner there's another street that is nothing but specialized florists, wreath shop after wreath shop, and a van is parked outside one of them, its shutter rolled up, and somebody says, "Hey you!" (one migrant worker is any migrant worker), summoning him to carry a wreath into the van, and another wreath, and yet another, and he gets in himself, pressed in the aromatic gap between layers of flowers, and the tailgate rolls down, and the dark van jolts off (the character inscribed on the center of each wreath signifies it's a gift for the dead), with relief he ceases for a while to be here, or now, or himself.

In the midst of the funeral gathering, a tidy smile, a politician rewinding in his head a joke he just shared with a civil servant (the one about the real estate developer and the prostitute), and what is there to regret, Qin had it coming, the timing of his passing suspiciously convenient for certain parties, he peers about, sorting Qin's allies from his enemies, though among the higher echelons the distinction is a fine one, a nod, a frown, who here did *not* have a motive to do away with Qin, who would have relished this gathering, squeezed the flesh of all his possible murderers, the ghost of the billionaire is working the room, as the politician stomps in his socks toward the shoe rack, and half-crouches, reaching out with hand and inquisitive foot toward where his brogues should be—but are not, an empty parking space, and wildly he looks around, speculating somebody might have moved them, or his memory might be at fault, one hypothesis as unacceptable as the other, then he understands what happened and he laughs, the impudence of the thief marching right into the funeral gathering, in the presence of bodyguards and security personnel, in the presence of some of the most powerful men in China, in the presence of death, well there's only one thing to be done, if a stranger steals your shoes you must steal a stranger's shoes, he inspects the many pairs dozing on the rack like delegates at a party congress, and he selects an excellent example, handmade, discreetly labeled Lobbs of London, and his toes squirm and settle inside them as if his feet had been crafted to suit these very objects, and he bows to do up the laces, he phones his chauffeur but there's no answer, he texts: "I'm on my way where are you" as he marches, elevated and authoritative, to the exterior marble steps, head fanning in order to pick out his own Audi, and he hears a voice behind him, "Excuse me, you've taken my shoes, Mr. Ximen! Excuse me, you've taken my Lobbs by mistake!," he descends, he kicks off the shoes, and why not the socks too, and barefoot as when he was a boy runs over the slimy, gritty surface of the city, and his Audi 12 rolls along keeping pace with him, and he pulls open the door and he too vanishes within its tinted glass as if he never existed.

Striding along in his borrowed brogues, limping along on his borrowed brogues, past a fruit man, past a man urging him to eat fish balls in boiling broth (Didn't somebody once construct a replica of the Great Wall out of fish ball skewers?) which reminds him of a joke that he cannot quite recall, the shading of it, its inner darkness, a sense of falling down and down through that darkness, and of his childhood, his mother's face dissolving as she tells him it, once upon a time a woman dropped a shoe down a well, "My child is in the well!" (a pun that works only in Sichuan, "shoe" and "child" being homophones in the local dialect) as he limps along the "traditional hutong" theme mall, a branch of an international coffee chain guarding it like a mastiff, and then into an actual hutong, narrow and winding, following the water-map in his head, and so into a zone marked for destruction, the character for "demolish" in red paint on several walls, builders' sand as if a beach, stray fluttery memories of months-old newspapers, dog shit, and he finds the promised house, seemingly unoccupied—yet on the door, angled and battered, he knocks, "Excuse me, you in there, excuse me, you if you're in there, somebody told me you're looking for shoes."

Meanwhile the gangster whose Lobbs were grabbed, shoeless on the steps, outraged, the outrage radiating from his heart, bangs fist on chest, trying to beat himself back to life, while his bodyguards support him on either side, holding him upright, and upright he collapses, immortalized in a rictus of hatred and envy, propped up next to the turtle-and-snake sculpture by the marble portal to the house where Qin is not either.

"What have you got?" in a high-pitched voice, the door opened a crack, an ancient face wrinkled yet softening as she admires the excellent brogues, the door creaks further but she does not allow him in, on the doorstep she kneels to evaluate the loot and so they haggle, they sniff each other's desperation, settling on a price of a hundred yuan—and she accepts the pair as if a gift, unlacing them, taking them off him, petting their hard-soft shell, and she gives him a pair of cloth shoes to wear instead, the kind anyone can get at an Everything for Two Yuan store, "When will I get paid?" "Ah, I'm only the intermediary, I pass the shoes on to a man from Shanghai," impelling him to exclaim, "Shanghai!" a city he never before had reason to name, while in Beijing dialect she replies, "You know what they say: when a wicked man dies in Beijing, he is reincarnated in Shanghai!" and he presses her, asking when he'll get his hundred yuan, and she tells him to come back for it at dusk, not long after dusk, and murmurs, "If you could lay your hands on more shoes like this . . ." hunger and pleading in her voice, she stands holding the brogues and she is short but full-length—scarlet stilettos, apron like a cobbler's, elasticated floral sleeve protectors, her dehydrated face is a wood ear mushroom, that still has spit enough in it to moisten her thumb, which rubs a mud crumb next to a welt—and he would find more for her too, he would do the old woman this service, though he dare not go back to the same funeral, in this city of millions there must be many deaths, many funerals, millions of lonesome shoes there for the taking.

Time is his to kill; he strolls backward and forward in time and space, the big city with its dense sour atmosphere and NO SMOKING, whereas in Sichuan the sky clear as water, the cigarettes homegrown, one for now and one for later tucked behind an ear, NO SPITTING but what else are you supposed to do with your phlegm, Beijing a bomb site or after an earthquake, he walks by what was once a school and what was once a restaurant and what was once a laundry . . . which is destined to become an elevator-rich glittery complex, a field with plums and peppers and in the far corner of it the stone grave marker by which he and his father burn death-money, not factory-made crisp paper, his ancestors make do with their local straw currency, palms together and bow three times, the city thickening as dusk approaches, a flock of clay-colored starlings weaves overheard, he wanders over to where he can climb on a low wall (half the hutong is demolished already) and peek inside her house, the interior explained by a single fluorescent blob, many pairs of shoes squared up on the otherwise empty cement floor, men's shoes and women's shoes, a line of shoes follow each other and turn! and back the other way to the end and turn! . . . like a line dance, like the way you plow a field, the shoes radiant and beautiful and expensive, and now the old woman appears, she caresses them and talks to them, in her passion not un-beautiful in her own right, she sits on a low stool and tries on now one pair, and now another, she sets a golden pump down on a sheet of sun-colored paper, and behind him a car eases up, a black Elantra, so he fades into the shadows, a wince in his bad ankle, the driver is talking into a cellphone and has a mustache, it looks as if it might be the cellphone that has the mustache, a bushiness shared between man and device, night pulls harder at its end, smoothing out the smog-shine, no individual star visible, the river that is the Milky Way having been dammed for the sake of a celestial hydroelectric project, and he is a fixed point, and Mustache is a fixed point and the old woman too, and now she lifts the very brogues he brought, temporarily his ears, into which she whispers.

This hutong is where she grows up, where she is a girl, where she is a young woman, poor but a beauty, where she turns down the marriage proposal of a high-ranking cadre and marries her sweetheart instead, and they have a daughter, and it is from here that husband and wife set out, day after day, year after year, to their assigned jobs as teachers, until one day he is denounced, she must denounce him, her husband is taken from her and her daughter does not forgive her, and she is married off to a former Red Guard, and she remains at her school until she is obliged to retire, and she takes care of her unloved second husband, who is frailer and frailer, supporting his remaining body with a stick, with two sticks, on braces, in a wheelchair, eventually only his eyes survive, goldfish in a bowl, and after decades of eating bitterness she is bereft and free (in her dreams history bites its tail and she is young and beautiful again) the one thing she wants and can still have is a splendid pair of shoes, she is as much entitled as any movie star or politician's wife, with her inheritance in hand she goes to a boutique in Nanluoguxiang and she splurges it all on one perfect pair of high heels and straps them on her feet and struts out and even as she steps onto the curb the fancy heels snap under her and the lying sole bends and the tongue shrugs, she's been sold a dud, and there's no going back, and in the repetitive chime from the crossing light she hears the chimed moral: *If a stranger steals your shoes, you must steal a stranger's shoes.*

The moral resonates, jolts him, he finds himself inside the house, confronting her: when will he get paid, is there really a dealer in Shanghai, what use to her are men's shoes unless she sells them, if she must have shoes why doesn't she go out and steal shoes for herself, and while she gropes for an answer he turns into his own stolen brogues, for there is no element in the human body, no curve or straightness, no continuity or discontinuity, no soft or hard, that the shoe does not possess— his cheeks are outsoles, his nose an upper, his forehead a welt, his eyes grommets through which the laces of his pupils wind, and his mouth is the secret insole which accuses her until she confesses there is no Shoe King in Shanghai, she's not a middleman but a collector, all is for herself, the shoes that thieves bring her, they're never the perfect ones, sometimes almost but not quite, so she keeps on waiting, keeps on hoping, and all she can pay him for shoes are shoes, "Take your pick," a fine tan lightweight lizardy pair, "Italian," soft against the skin, as she narrates the legend of the Great Bell of Beijing, how the bronze casters at the foundry couldn't get the thing to come out quite right and if it failed they would all be executed, and as a terrible last resort they threw a smith's infant daughter into the molten metal, leaving her tiny embroidered slippers behind, and ever since, when the clapper strikes the bell, it sings out *Shoe! Shoe!*, the girl pining for her missing footwear.

She locks eyes and he is the image of her first husband on their wedding day, she is a lovely and innocent and vigorous girl with all her life ahead of her, while he looking through her looks through the stained window: Mustache still in the Elantra, then a second unmarked car drifts up, and a third, and Mustache and the men in the other cars get out, and he ollies into a possible future and back again, he stutters upright, shouting, "Get out! Get out at once!," the old woman stunned as if photographed, among the serried shoes a giantess looming over city blocks, he seizes her arm, a frail corn stalk, "Escape!" willing them both minutes into the future and into the alleyway behind her house at the same time as police churn inside of it, their big black dumb shoes on the treasured shoes, a ram kicks over its bucket, and at the end of the alley a whirly-light car pulls up, more police pouring out of that, he presses the old woman against the dim, crumbly old-sloganed wall, his arms on either side of her, shielding her, and in order to hide her face and his he places his on hers, they pass for lovers, ignored by police who stampede past, they must kiss, they must be kissed, they must become each other, his head-top the honey-smelling fontanel of a baby, her ancient saliva a water that is strangely dry from the bottom of a well or something like a raindrop on the tongue, once when he was a boy he kissed a ewe just to learn what it would taste like: it was straw and soil and boiled cloud in the mouth.

After the police have left, the new migrant and the old Beijinger go back inside—all the shoes, every last piece, gone, the place an echoing emptiness, these two the only survivors in the devastated city. Behold a doorstop, a chunk of ignored granite—older than China, igneous, all but unchanging—ringed by a smog of soft transitory beings.

He wakes—some dream of a vague palace, he was mounted on a throne of sorts, a cloud-capped mountain—it is dawn and he is alone and cold and almost naked, alien items clinging to his feet, his clothing scattered to the close horizon, and whatever happened here no more or less real than his work on the skyscraper windows, than his accompanying a flock along a poor-pastured mountainside, in the course of a day, without any prompting, gradually the flock buoys itself to higher and higher ground, and more of his dream comes back to him, how he made love to a fox spirit with an eight-sided face who cloaked herself in a virgin's painted skin, he harvests his shirt and pants, groping the pockets, money has not multiplied miraculously, the bubble teeters in the spirit level, a flock breaks into a granary, the foolish creatures eat and eat till their stomachs bloat, the only hope being for the shepherd to plunge his knife in—a terrible wind redolent of fermented corn and bowels blows him out the cracked building, its windows a void, DEMOLISH on its door, and through the doomed hutong till he emerges blinking and flailing in some side street of greater Qianmen, workers with complexions the no-hue of fermented mung bean juice off to their jobs, on the far side of the complicated intersection zany with stoplights and car horns there is a scenery wall, he staggers through a gap in it and men from his village grouped around a fire fueled with scrap wood and garbage scarcely bother to grunt a greeting, he takes off his fabulous shoes and rests them atop the fire, and by the kitchen tent there is a pair of scuffed army boots that will do, he is served soy milk and fried dough, the foreman clocks him in and, his limp vanished, he ascends the building-to-be, to the eighteenth floor of the skyscraper that is already a glory and is destined to become more and more glorious until such time as it will be demolished to be replaced by a yet more magnificent skyscraper, here to install more and more panes. Elsewhere the shoes tumble off the pyre, their glow not so bright in the average sunshine, and walk across the site and out the entrance, and, flaming steadily, emitting a stinking smoke, alongside the many busy Beijingers with things on their mind, the fire-shoes continue their saunter along Qianmen Dajie, unobtrusive in the city that has known it all before and will accept even this.

*

Once the police retrieve the haul of stolen shoes, it remains to return them to their original owners; there is a notice in a local newspaper, and an announcement on the radio, and several Residents Committees are informed, and the Public Security Bureau website has a link anyone can click on: Turn up at such-and-such a location at such-and-such a time, and your long-missing property might be waiting for you.

The municipality operates on the Cinderella system. Young and old, poor and less poor, native and migrant, stand in a line that ribbons and twists back on itself on the sidewalk outside a recreations building, and in fours or sixes, men to the right, women to the left, are allowed into what was and will be again a basketball court, where, studious, they process up and down, poring over the array of shoes, attending to them—the bargain being: if it clutches in the right way, if it seeks to meld with the foot, if it recognizes you, then you consent to recognize it. Some trudge on; some gasp with pleasure—past and future sides of the same coin—at recovering what went astray at a funeral or a whorehouse or a changing room at a gym . . . and some never had anything stolen but are here on the make—*Will you be mine, will I be yours, what kind of China might we belong in?*

NETWORKING

You could almost think you were in a foreign country. Once this was a treaty port, and there remain a number of European buildings, pretty and absurd. A pleasure steamer goes past, so close you feel you could reach out and touch it, with tourists raising phones to capture the beach. Farther out is a chemical transporter, bizarrely un-ship-like in form, being composed of reservoirs and tentacle-like pipes; NO SMOKING painted in characters larger than the name of the ship itself, and a lone seaman is on deck, leaning against a railing, smoking.

Qin observes all this. He turns and climbs over the rocky foreshore, and encounters, coming the other way, a younger man, Nie, wearing a T-shirt with English words on it. It seems one or the other will have to step aside, but actually neither does, for there is a vendor drawing their attention. He is cross-legged on a sheet of white vinyl; his DVD emits jaunty music while a paper cut-out of a cartoon dog, upright on the plastic, jigs in tempo. How does this work? What hidden mechanism makes it possible? "Buy one for your children! Five yuan each, three for ten yuan!" and, imploring Qin, "Buy one for your mistress!"

It is Nie who crouches, and gets six, all different, the dog in addition to other creatures. "My girls will love this!"

"Girls?"

"Twins. In August they'll turn five."

"Ah, twin girls! How cute! Nature helps you evade the one-child policy. I have a daughter too, but she would not like this." While the vendor is calling out to some other tourist, Qin explains, "It is a con. The animals won't dance when you take them home."

"They won't?"

"Look carefully. There is a fishing line sewn through the cutout on display. He jiggles it with his thumb. The dog doesn't dance just because the music plays. How could it? Do you believe in magic?"

Nie takes off his glasses, and wipes them on his T-shirt. "Why didn't you tell me before I bought them?"

Qin smiles. He presents a business card; the address is a prestigious district of Beijing. Nie is not carrying his cards, no matter, he is an accountant employed by a third-tier provincial city. They shake hands, each taking a formal pleasure in saying the other's name. Qin writes the information into his smartphone. He has an intuition in these matters: as soon he spied the accountant he knew what kind of person he must be.

"The weather is beautiful," Qin says.

"It is indeed beautiful."

"What's the weather like, where you come from?"

"The summer is hot. My twins love coming here. The Qingdao breeze is so refreshing."

The conversation is clichéd and stilted, as it should be. This is how one approaches a person like Nie. Qin has perhaps never before encountered such a perfect example of the type.

"Your hotel is good?" Qin says. "And not too expensive?"

"Ai, we're paying the high-season price."

"I have many friends here. Next time I will negotiate you a discount. Where are your lovely twins?"

"They're in the hotel with my wife."

"My wife and daughter are asleep in the hotel. They prefer to get up late." In fact his wife is home in Beijing, and his daughter . . . well he certainly hopes she's in Beijing too. Last month she took off without telling him with some school friends to Shanghai—all paid for on his credit card. He's on his own in Qingdao, here to meet up with old clients, and, as always, looking out for new.

"My wife chose the hotel. She found it on the internet," Nie says. "Her cousin lives in Beijing; perhaps you know him? Their family name is Kong, the same as Confucius."

Qin quotes the opening of *The Analects*: *"How delightful to meet friends from afar."*

Nearby, the paper animal seller stands with his back to them; he urinates, calligraphing the rocks. Qin and Nie walk along a concrete path, from where they have a view of the skyscrapers in the business district across the bay. A sweating fellow is grilling a rack of cuttlefish. Qin offers to buy one for his companion. The cuttlefish are tricky to handle, since they are big and chewy and coated with sweet brown sauce. The men each hold up a skewered cuttlefish, as if gesturing with hand puppets.

How pleasant to grumble about one's job, while on vacation! Nie chatters away, and Qin grunts sympathetically. They lean forward so as to bite into their cuttlefish without dripping sauce on their shirts.

"Delicious," Qin says.

"Yes, delicious."

And now Qin makes his move. As he speaks, he gestures with his food, and one might imagine his half-eaten cuttlefish is doing the talking. It is a practiced speech yet subtly modified, with many commendations of the accountant's desire to provide for his family. What Qin suggests is a simple business proposition, with no risk to either party, a win-win situation. It might seem unusual to somebody from a provincial city, but he can confidently assert that by Beijing standards it is considered acceptable. In conclusion he raises his cuttlefish. "May we have a fruitful cooperation!" But Nie presents his own skewered cuttlefish as if to parry a thrust. "According to the reg-g-g-ulations . . ." He stammers, like the legendary courtier who disagreed with the emperor, and his regional accent becomes stronger. "Thank you, Mr. Qin, goodbye." The young man turns and scurries inland, leaving a trail of sauce behind him. Qin calls after him, "It was a pleasure, Accountant Nie." An elegant woman saunters by attached to a Pomeranian. A street cleaner stares at the tourists; she goes on sweeping the ground with her plastic broom.

Qin sighs. Where did he go wrong? What else could he have done? Now if he'd had longer with Nie, taken him out for a drink, told him stories of other middle-ranking officials whom he'd helped with their financial worries. . . . He can only hope he'll encounter him again; in his experience of business relationships, they are often like a series of seemingly independent stories that turns out in the end to make up one grand narrative.

He checks his phone. Messages from his secretary and his lawyer and business contacts. . . . He dispatches a dozen carefully worded replies. He was a child during the Cultural Revolution; he remembers orations and anthems and chants, extravagant praise swerving into fiery denunciation. Stability is not the natural state of things, he has learned, we strive to maintain it. Also a voicemail from his wife; nothing from his daughter. He calls his daughter, and gets only the answering beep. "Xiaxia, this is Daddy. I'm at the airport, about to fly home. Where are you? I love you."

*

Remember me? No, that won't do. Or: *I came all this way to see you.* Definitely not. Qin puzzles how best to phrase it. It's not quite the case that he came just for this—he arranged to do business in the provincial capital the previous day—but he's here on the hunt. In honor of the Mid-Autumn Festival, a celebration is taking place in the main square in Nie's city. A troupe of middle-aged women in orange uniform are banging cymbals and marching in a circle. A carrion crow on a lamppost rocks to the beat. The master of ceremonies barks into his microphone. On the stage, four sturdy girls stand in a row. Three smaller girls climb on top, balancing on the shoulders of those beneath. And now a pair of petite girls in tutus, identical twins, ascends to the very apex. The twins hoist a national flag between them. Their grin stands for determination overcoming fear. The crow flaps to a ginkgo tree, which sheds yellow leaves. The human pyramid presents itself as a perspective drawing: the twins might be full-size women, high up and far away. While the crowd is applauding Qin throws his cigarette on the ground. He glances from side to side. Their father must be here. On Nie's homepage he was boasting about this performance for weeks. *You look familiar. Haven't I seen you before?* No, that won't do either.

But in the end it is Nie who notices him first. "Ah, what a pleasure!" He turns to the woman next to him, the perky big-eyed type, "Mr. Qin is a businessman from Beijing. We met in Qingdao. Didn't I tell you about him?"

Qin shakes hands with Nie and with his wife. On his home turf Nie is more confident. He seems to have forgotten the disagreeable element of their last meeting; he has a selective memory, as we all do. He is proud to show off his connection with an important person from the capital. And he doesn't seem surprised at Qin's presence here either, as if taking it for granted that the whole world passes through this city, sooner or later.

Qin sticks fairly close to the truth. "I was in the vicinity, and I noticed on the civic website that your lovely girls would be performing. How could I fail to view them?" He leans close to the wife and murmurs, "I understand you're a direct descendant of Confucius."

She gazes past the visitor's shoulder. "Our city is famous for its moon cakes." She goes to make sure her daughters put on their coats.

The sun peeks through the clouds, along with a touch of rain. Qin says, "Would you like a Zhongnanhai? They have such a rich aroma." The men retreat under an awning to smoke. All around them, citizens are meeting up and gossiping in hearty voices. The microphone blurts intermittently. On the stage, men and women in quaint costumes are taking part in a traditional dance associated with the region, and musicians play, and here and there in the square young couples dance in their own various manners.

The men face each other. "What an excellent performance! Your twins reached the sky!"

"Indeed, they reached the sky. Does your daughter perform gymnastics too?"

"My daughter has many talents."

Their smoke gathers between them.

Nie takes off his glasses in order to rub his eyes.

"Are your eyes sore?" Qin says.

"My eyes are a little sore."

"Sometimes I suffer from allergies myself."

"I'm thinking of having the operation, where they cut your eyes with a laser, but a friend of mine had it done, and his eyesight actually got worse."

"I also am considering the operation." A white lie—for the operation helps only with myopia. Qin is astigmatic in his right eye and slightly presbyopic in his left; without glasses, winking, he can see what's going on in the distance. He rubs his better eye, to keep Nie company.

The scene shimmers and distorts. Qin can see only Nie, Nie only Qin; there is nothing but the two of them, surrounded by chaos.

The band plays on, and feet beat on the resonant earth, and there are stray words from many conversations and a roar that might be an airplane passing over.

Nie puts his glasses on, and his complicated world snaps back. His wife returns with the excited twins.

Qin makes an effort to focus. He holds himself with care, like an alcoholic taking pains to pass for sober. "I'm staying at the White Swan Hotel, Accountant Nie. Perhaps you could come round for a drink later? Waah you're so pretty! And you too! You're hardworking and talented! How you honor your parents!"

The twins hug their mother's hips; she pats their heads, and their father too crouches to congratulate them; the family is a callisthenic display in its own right. The outsider is like that giant whose legs were taken to be tree trunks, too massive to be visible.

There is a long wait for the toilets. Qin flashes a document with an impressive-looking stamp, and jumps to the front of the line. The air freshener implies an evergreen forest, and Tchaikovsky is piped in. Afterward he admires himself in the mirror. He is not physically vain. He knows his face is sucked-in and not quite symmetrical, as if a drawstring were tugged too hard. He was born in the Year of the Tiger, and there is a tigerish pattern of wrinkles on his forehead like the character for "king": 王. He can use his appearance to serve his interests: to cow an opponent, and to charm; a touch of hideousness adds piquancy, like vinegar in the soup.

That evening, in the hotel bar, the men drink scotch. The bartender presses on them a brand with a purple and gold label, but Qin insists on Glenfiddich. He assures Nie he's done similar deals before, with many clients in many provinces, and everything has always gone smoothly. (Not quite true. One of his clients was fired. Another was very nearly arrested, and Qin had to pay to hush it up. A third is in jail, but that was on account of a separate embezzlement, unrelated to Qin's activities.)

And consider the twins' future! Nie owes it to them to broaden his horizons!

The fundamental idea is straightforward. In any organization there is always cash that needs to be invested on a short-term basis. Naturally the interest paid would be low, let's say 2%. And often it's necessary to borrow money on a short-term basis too, at quite a high rate, let's say 12%. Now, if Nie were to arrange for the municipal authorities to borrow a million yuan from an investment company controlled by Qin, and to deposit a million yuan into another investment company controlled by Qin, why that's a profit of 100,000 yuan right there, to be split between them 70–30! Of course, that's only illustrative: the actual deal would be much more complex, hard to audit; irregular amounts would be borrowed and lent at various rates for various periods. As Mao said—or was it Confucius?—*We think too small, like the frog at the bottom of the well. He thinks the sky is only as big as the top of the well.*

Nie sips. "You make it sound so easy!"

"It is easy."

"Why doesn't everybody do it?"

"Oh, but everybody does it, all the successful people, I mean. Not exactly this method, but something like this. Tell me about your boss. How does he afford his limousine? Who pays for his beach vacation in Hainan, his gambling trip to Macau, his wife's jewelry? How come he has such a luscious young mistress?"

"I really don't think—"

"Ah, maybe your boss is an exception. I wasn't speaking personally. But look around you. The people who enjoy a good life, they didn't get where they are by sitting on their ass and obeying every petty regulation!"

As Qin inveighs, he considers that he sounds like his own daughter. She's a great believer in breaking rules. Ever since she was fifteen she's been going to nightclubs using a fake ID. Her school report is awful. If she were in a Chinese school, she'd be in serious trouble. But they live in a gated community in the north of Beijing, near the airport, and she attends an international school. The school has a strict policy of not accepting Chinese students, but an exception was made, in return for a generous donation. His own teachers used to recite, "Study hard and improve daily" (he came from a modest background and struggled to get an education), but as far as she's concerned school is an opportunity for fun and *networking*—a favorite English word of hers that seems Chinese in as much as it's composed of two characters. She's a junior in high school. She's got it all figured out. She plans to go to the University of Southern California and become a movie producer. "America's got talent and China's got money," she likes to say. She's going to persuade Chinese billionaires to invest in Hollywood. She'll take her cut.

The fact is, Qin has had several close shaves. He's been investigated by the authorities, but so far he's managed to wriggle out of it. He "covers the mountain with mists and clouds," as the saying goes. He operates through offshore investment vehicles. He always denies personal responsibility, but if necessary he agrees to pay compensation anyway. Some of his clients, though, they get greedy, they overreach. Sooner or later, he fears, a scandal will break; maybe he'll only be peripherally involved, but the authorities will be under pressure to lop a tall tree. But it seems to him that his corruption (if that is how it is to be defined) is outside himself—it existed thousands of years in the past, and will exist thousands of years in the future—he can take neither praise nor blame. He's less concerned for himself than for his daughter. If he falls, then she won't be able to study abroad, and her dreams will never come true. Let him just stay out of harm's way for a few more years, he prays, another decade. He thinks of the zodiacal animals, a heavenly menagerie; if he lives through the full cycle again, it'll be more than he expects. By then her career will be established, and nobody in America will care if a producer's father is locked up in a Chinese prison, or executed, in fact she might use it to advantage. She'll hint that her father was a dissident, persecuted for his commitment to democratic values. Personally Qin is happier in his own country—vacationing in New York or London or Tokyo only when his wife and daughter insist—but he accepts that his daughter will be a citizen of the world. And in certain moods he's an optimist. There's every chance, provided he plays his cards right, that he'll rise to greater and greater heights, he'll be too big to fail, investors will shower his daughter with money in order to get in with him. What he hopes, above all, is that she has a child. He's no stickler for tradition—Xiaxia can give him a grandson or a granddaughter; she can marry a big-nosed Westerner, for all he cares—but one way or another he wants his lineage to continue. The contemplation of his own mortality consoles him.

"Cheers!" Qin says in English, leaning forward with his whisky raised.

*

"I'll phone you when I'm done," Qin tells his chauffeur.

Snow is shunted in heaps and the sky is heavy. The snuffling chauffeur closes his eyes with his mouth open, as if spelled into a deep sleep. The dashboard ornament is a plastic sunflower that raises and lowers its leaves perpetually. Qin advised Nie to admit nothing; there is no reason to panic. But the man has come all the way to Beijing just in order to meet with him. He can't refuse. Right now he needs a drink.

He's in a foreign language bookstore, the Bookworm. It's not just the words that are foreign, the very shapes of the books and magazines, the designs of the covers, come from far away. For good luck he buys a hardback in English—*Gets inside the heads of people living in China today,* declares the blurb; difficult to tell whether it's fact or fiction. He goes to the bar, where a red-haired bartender greets him in Mandarin, and he orders a double Glenfiddich. He feels safer here, half in China and half abroad. Sometimes an outsider can understand us in a way we do not understand ourselves. His wife sees a psychoanalyst, who sits in silence while she talks.

Nie comes in, and Qin realizes he's picked the wrong location. The idea was to bring Nie somewhere he'd be uncomfortable, to give Qin an advantage. But Nie is more than uncomfortable enough already. His face is haggard and his trouser cuffs are soaked. He's unused to this climate; probably he walked from the subway. What if the accountant were to rant, to assign blame, to confess in public? Many here would not get it, guessing this to be a quarrel between boss and employee, or between father and son, or between lovers; others would relish every word.

Qin springs up and seizes Nie by the elbow. "I'm taking

you somewhere more private." As they leave, a couple is murmuring, *"Je t'aime."* His daughter taught him the expression on the Air France flight. Throughout their stay at the hotel on the Champs Elysées, and at the Louvre, and in various department stores, he never had occasion to use that phrase, or indeed any of his minimal French, though quite possibly Xiaxia, strolling by moonlight along the banks of the Seine, spoke it and had it spoken to her. As pretty as his daughter is now, so was his wife in her youth. What did she see in him: Did she perceive, beneath the surface, some kind of beauty? On their wedding night, she conceived. The timing was wrong; he had a career to pursue. Four years later, Xiaxia was born. He has always given his wife everything she's entitled to. He is faithful—not that sex was ever the center of their marriage; the world holds other desires, far more potent.

The chauffeur steers toward the curb, and, yawning, double-parks. The Audi has an adaptive suspension system; when Qin is at the back, his ride is smooth. But he believes that as soon as he gets out the chauffeur switches the suspension to sporty mode, and as if it were his own takes the vehicle for a spin, feeling every pothole and bump and irregularity of Beijing.

The passengers tramp around a snow drift, their track already flattened and darkened by generations of pedestrians. They enter the wholesale market—multiple levels of consumer goods. They take a series of escalators to the food court on the top floor. Here, at least, it's most unlikely Qin would encounter anybody he knows.

Neither is hungry.

They sit on plastic chairs. A not very clean table is between them. Two cups of water, left behind by previous diners, stake out the surface. There's a NO SMOKING sign, and indeed nobody is smoking.

"Help me," Nie says.

Qin tips his head back and sucks through his teeth. He feels an urge to charge forward, head-butting the accountant till their glasses collide and smash. How ugly Nie is, with his squinty little face and his fading hair! How ugly Nie's wife is too! How ugly the twins: he's never seen such ugly girls in his life! What a perfectly ugly family! How he hopes Nie does not go through with the operation: it would be horrible to confront his naked eyes.

Meanwhile Nie is rambling on, stammering and repeating himself, descanting on the suspicions of his boss, his fear the municipality might appoint an outside auditor. . . . In reaction to this frantic talk, Qin grows in power. He has never been so sure of himself in his life. He stands and raises an arm as if saluting from a podium, and it is his turn to speak. He proclaims this is a problem that will pass. It is not important in the grand scheme of things. The paper trail can be obscured by a further series of transactions, more debits, more credits, more borrowings, more loans.... We are facing danger, yes, there will be further dangers in the months and years to come, but so long as we stand together, united in the face of adversity, a glorious future lies ahead!

ELVIS HAS LEFT BEIJING

They were sisters, but of course they were not *sisters*. (That would be contrary to government policy.) Their families had lived side by side in the Shijingshan District of Beijing for many generations. They were born during the same calendar year, but in different traditional years—Linlin, a month older, was a Monkey and Feifei a Rooster. Perhaps that made the difference.

When she was twelve, Linlin had her first period and a month later so did Feifei. Linlin kissed a boy when she was sixteen; a month later, Feifei. They went through various teenage enthusiasms together, too—their calligraphy phase, their boy band phase, their phase of crushes on other girls. On the parapet of a warehouse destined for demolition the spray-painted slogan appeared: WOMAN'S DESTINY IS TO RULE OVER MAN; they accomplished this when they were seventeen, the year they both lost their virginity.

To everyone's surprise they scored high on the national exam and got into college. They decided they would take their future seriously. They had a gift for languages; they watched American movies and British TV series, and haunted the English Corner to ask questions of native speakers.

On graduating they both accepted a position at a multi-national company (not the same one). Their work was a little humdrum. A more urgent topic engrossed them: Whom should they choose as their first real boyfriend? He'd be somebody more senior than themselves, earning a decent salary, aiming high. But should he be Chinese or a foreigner? They listed the advantages of each.

Chinese:
- Understands your background.
- You understand his.
- Can meet his parents.
- Shares common goals.

Foreigner:
- Enchanted by you.
- Thinks you're beautiful. (If you have any flaws, he's unaware of them.)
- Makes bitchy girls jealous of you. ("What does he see in her?")
- Lets you get away with whatever you want.

They sat in a fast-food restaurant near Qianmen and giggled about it. Should they two-time their imaginary boyfriends, sampling one of each type? But they weren't that kind of girl. No, what made sense was for the two sisters, between them, to do what neither could alone. Linlin took a sachet of soy sauce and one of ketchup. She held them behind her back, shuffling them to and fro. She stretched out her fists for Feifei to choose from.

Feifei tensed. She felt—which was unusual—envy, though she didn't know what Linlin would be getting that she herself would not.

A tap on the right fist.

It opened.

Ketchup.

Linlin saw a tremble on her sister's lips, a disappointment. "You know," she said generously, "You can choose your own fate." She opened her other fist now—and Feifei reached out and grasped the familiar soy sauce, and pressed it, like a doll pillow, against her cheek.

So Linlin's destiny was ketchup. The sisters felt they could live with the decision. From here on, they understood, their true education would begin. They bought a single order of french fries, sharing it between them, each dipping the fries into her own sauce.

For her first foreigner, Linlin picked Andy; she might as well go for somebody who speaks the Queen's English. He was from Newcastle-upon-Tyne and had arrived in China two weeks previously, to work at her company. He was skinny with auburn curls and the whitest of complexions; she could never decide if he was very beautiful or very ugly. For his part, he was eager to have a Chinese girlfriend to "show him the ropes." She thought she might celebrate by giving herself an English nickname—Linda, perhaps? But Andy talked her out of it. "Nothing wrong with Lin," he said, "It's my dental hygienist's name."

"My friends call me Linlin."

"Even better," he said, ogling her breasts. "Double your pleasure, double your fun!"

As well as improving her English she learned Western customs. (For example, Andy drank a glass of cold water with every meal.) The sex was not bad; she could be less self-conscious with him, knowing that he fancied her not as an individual but as a race. She asked him to speak English idioms in bed ("You're a nice bit of skirt!") but this embarrassed him, and she had to settle for his repertory of grunts.

She confided all this in her sister, who asked, "Those folds in the eyelids, do you think they're attractive, Big Sister?"

"His eyes look like belly buttons!" And the sisters laughed.

After they'd been together a fortnight, one Sunday Andy took Linlin to a pub in Wudaoku, *The Three Feathers,* to show her off to his mates. It was fascinating to be among Englishmen en masse. The more beer they drank, the redder their cheeks became. Some bloke with sideburns persuaded her to have a bite of his Yorkshire pudding, which was, to her surprise, delicious. She could generally follow their chatter;

their indispensable word was *wanker*—an insult, but also a term of friendship (much as, she thought, Chinese men address each other as "turtle egg"). Male camaraderie, even in the most genial of forms, always has a whiff of eros and of danger. There was gossip about somebody's old school friend who'd been found dead in a hotel room; they laughed at this, but then, Westerners laugh at almost anything.

The pub filled up with more foreigners, and some Chinese too, and she discovered this was not a random gathering but an event organized by the Beijing chapter of the Hash House Harriers. "Drinkers with running problems," Sideburns explained with a smirk. They meet every Sunday, each time in a different neighborhood. They jog together, stopping for booze along the way. To make it more fun, one person reconnoiters ahead carrying a bag containing flour, with a tennis ball in it which he bounces as he goes, to leave a trail. Then off in pursuit the Hashers run.

"Is there a prize for coming first?" she asked. "Do some people get lost?"

"Only one way to find out," said Andy.

It was an exhilarating and exotic experience. A typical Hasher was white and male, from Britain or the Commonwealth. There was a quota of Americans and of Europeans too, even Indians and a Nigerian, and she was far from unique: several men had brought their Chinese girlfriends. (She small-talked to these others in English, which was like acting in a play.) Jealously she noticed Andy staring at somebody's cleavage stickered *HELLO! I'M MEIXIN YANG!* (the name in back-to-front order, the way it's done in English, as if the individual could take precedence over the family) but, far from flirting, the woman quizzed him about the accounting procedures in his company.

The jog began, some loping athletically, others panting and shuffling. Those near the front shouted, "On, on!" while the "slow coaches" trailed after.

She and Andy came back the following Sunday, and almost every Sunday through that dusty, cool spring. It was a ritual; something to look forward to. In other respects Andy was not so satisfactory (he drank too much, and then he was no good in bed) but the Hash linked them. She became a familiar face; the men collectively flirted with her. "Is Lin lean?" they'd ask, and she'd respond, coping with the vowels, "Yes, Lin's lean." For some reason, this was considered funny.

Singing was an important part of the Hash—reminding her of her time in the Young Pioneers. For example, if a woman had small breasts (all Chinese women were deemed to fit into this category) the men would serenade her:

She's all right
She's all right

She's got no tits
But she's all right!

whereas if hers were large:

She's all right
She's all right
She's got a great big rack
But she's too white!

By the time the Hash reached this drunken, uproarious stage, she'd grab Andy's hand and prepare to go home.

In April, quite suddenly, Andy departed. (He got a posting in Lagos.) At the farewell Hash his mates sang, to the tune of "Auld Lang Syne,"

Fuck off! You wank! Fuck off! You wank!
Fuck off! You wank! Fuck off!
Fuck off! You wank! Fuck off! You wank!
Fuck off! You wank! Fuck off!

She described all this to her sister, who put her hand over her mouth and smiled. "They are foolish. But you're improving your English, and you're making connections. That will help you find a better boyfriend, Big Sister."

Linlin remained in the Hash and found her subsequent dates through it. Paul from Northern Ireland. Brian the New Zealander (their big quarrel came when she informed him the kiwi was originally a Chinese fruit, and he said, "You people think you invented everything!"). Jean-Phi from Belgium. Finally, in July, George, an American.

The younger sister had a less varied love life. A month after Linlin went on her first Hash, Feifei accepted an invitation from a manager in her company, Chen Rong. (He was in Compliance, and liaised with her section on a regular basis.) They went for a stroll in Ritan Park after work. He was a short man with glasses and an odd speech defect, pronouncing *sh* like *s*, which (though he was from an old Beijing family) made him sound as if he was from somewhere like Taiwan.

A week later, she had Yunnanese crossing-the-bridge noodles with him.

A week later, the first kiss.

A week later, she met his mother, with whom he lived.

And the following week Feifei asked Rong his dream. He said he wanted to be promoted within the company, and one day reach a senior position in the Beijing office. According to the internet: *People born in the Year of the Rooster are virtuous, constant, and financially lucky. An excellent choice of partner would be a person born in the Year of the Ox. . . .* And Chen Rong was an Ox!

It wasn't till June that Linlin (who was then in the process of breaking up with Jean-Phi) got a text from Feifei: she and Rong were in a hotel near the Great Wall. Feifei was in provocative lingerie that her sister had helped her choose, and Rong was taking a preliminary shower. Linlin texted back at once: *Good luck!* An hour later, the reply: *It was amazing!* followed by a string of emoticons to express the Little Sister's delight.

The sisters tried to switch from text to speech, but the reception was poor; they could only hear fragments of each other. "I'm losing you," they kept crying. And when they next met, the following evening, beaming Feifei announced that Rong had proposed marriage. And how romantically! He'd taken their mingled pubic hairs and pressed them on the steamed-up bathroom mirror in the shape of the double-happiness sign! It turned out that on top of his salary he had an extra income (he supplied business analysis to a banker named Qin) and useful family connections (his maternal uncle was a high-ranking cadre). He owned an apartment in Haidian; the housing market was soaring; it was sure to be a solid investment. The sisters hugged; they jumped up and down together, till Feifei got a nosebleed, which, as Linlin pointed out, signifies passionate love, in the case of cartoon characters anyway.

*

George was a step up on Linlin's previous boyfriends; though no older, he seemed more mature. He'd worked for the federal government. "In the US, China's the whipping boy, but you get a different perspective when you're actually here." He was making a determined effort to learn Mandarin. His career was advancing too: so many opportunities to practice international law, which would be impossible in America. She didn't officially move in with him, but stayed in his apartment in Dongzhimen most nights, shortening her commute. He referred to his favorite kind of sex with her as the Foreign Corrupt Practices Act—a pun that he explained at length.

Like her, too, he perceived himself as an outsider at the Hash. "It's like a Brit having the hots for a Hollywood star, or being a fan of the Yankees—he loves them just as much as we do, but he knows they're not his." A consideration might have been that he was worried about his waistline (he was a devotee of a diet which permits protein and fat but forbids carbohydrates; his standby was steak) and puffed when he ran.

He narrated the myth of origin. In colonial Kuala Lumpur, in the 1930s, a group of British accountants used to lunch every day at their club, which they nicknamed the Hash House; they took it on themselves to run to and from it. The founder of the Hash House Harriers died in Singapore during the War. Afterward the organization was re-founded, and spread among expats around the world. Linlin had a paternal great-uncle whose black-and-white photograph was on the family shrine; she knew practically nothing about him except that he too had been killed by the Japanese. Now the Hash didn't seem quite so exotic. She envisioned the ghost of Great-Uncle Xie, tipsy and cheery, scampering along with the Hashers.

Once upon a time, a man in Shanghai was cycling past a residential building when a fire extinguisher fell on him, injuring his shoulder. It must have come from one of the apartments, but there was no knowing which. He sued, and all the residents had to pay their share of his compensation.

This was a precedent for a case George was dealing with. A client of his, an American company with a subsidiary in Guangdong, operated a factory that might or might not have been polluting the water table. If his client's factory wasn't the cause, it was one of a number of local factories. The nearby villagers were suing the owners of all the factories. George was trying to get the case transferred to American jurisdiction, in which case (he was confident) his client would win.

"Frankly, my client is in the right, under local law, too, but you can't rely on the judges to rule accordingly. You know what people say: in America the law is an .exe file, but in China it's a .doc file!"

"Ah, those poor peasants!" Linlin said. "Ah, that poor man with the broken shoulder!"

George thrust his chin out, and practiced his address to the court on her, turning from side to side, advancing and retreating, almost dancing in his effort to convince. "... *Byrne versus Boadle* ... *Larson versus St. Francis Hotel* ... *Res ipsa loquitur* ... *Respondeat superior* ..."

She left him at it, and went to bed.

Linlin, seated between her boyfriend and her mother, felt strangely distanced from the actual wedding, having imagined it so often. The wedding organizer fluttered around like a moth. The lazy Susan kept rotating, with a choice of drinks. Toast followed toast. "Lucky! Lucky!" George cried loud in Mandarin, as he downed shots of maotai. Feifei appeared in three successive dresses—Western-style white, traditional red, and finally a sky-blue qipao. Linlin mimed brushing away tears as bride and groom bowed to Heaven and Earth, their parents, and each other.

The culmination was the screening of a video. Pretty Feifei and her geeky-looking groom romance each other in different costumes and settings, from the Song Dynasty to a futuristic space station. Linlin, appropriately costumed, appears in the background of every incarnation.

Linlin was promoted in late summer; now that she had an assistant to help her, she had more free time. She joined a gym. Regularly after work she exercised on the running machine. She gazed into the video screen, and as she ran her avatar ran through Paris or Venice or the Forbidden City.

Feifei joined too, and quite often the sisters met up there; they and their avatars jogged side by side.

One afternoon in October they went after exercise to the rooftop refreshment area, which featured a traditional hexagonal pavilion. "You've been working out so hard, Big Sister. You have such a slim figure."

Linlin felt she should return the compliment, but actually Feifei was looking a little fat. "Remember when we were seventeen, and we shoplifted a pair of red shoes with high pointy heels. I took one shoe and you took the other shoe. Whatever happened to the shoes?"

"It was that punk boy who egged us on." Feifei smiled. They'd gone to a punk concert once by mistake, thinking it was a boy band. The punk had taken both their virginities.

"Men! Who needs them?" Linlin said. "Apart from your Rong, of course."

Hung on the wall was a painting of the God of Wealth who, from Feifei's perspective, seemed to be perched on Linlin's shoulders; you could interpret it as the god riding the woman, or the woman marching off with the god. Feifei remembered how as girls Linlin used to lead her into daring adventures, but looking back perhaps it was the Rooster who'd really been in charge: by expressing her own hesitation prompting the Monkey to show off? She rested her hand on her sister's. "It's George, isn't it?"

Linlin spat it out. "He moved back to Washington. He

got a job as a lobbyist." She mimicked him, "We can learn a lot from you people." The irony being that it was a cliché for Chinese politicians to give America that backhanded compliment.

Loyal Feifei said, "I'm sure there's a good man for you ... in my office ... or we could look online ... or ..."

Linlin had been serially monogamous since starting her job. "Maybe I'll take a break from dating, for a while. I should concentrate on my career."

"Yes, maybe a little break," Feifei said, rather too quickly.

"And it's true," Linlin said, agreeing with what hadn't been said, "you do learn something from your relationships, even the lousy ones."

The drinks arrived: ginger-lemon and peach. The sisters sank their broad straws into each other's drink, sucking up the chewy tapioca pearls, tasting alternatives. From where they sat they had a view over Beijing. The current skyscrapers seemed architectural models for future, vaster skyscrapers.

"My company lost a big contract. A whole division was shut down and many people were fired," Feifei gossiped. "And a secretary in my office got engaged. She's lactose-intolerant, and her fiancé is lactose-intolerant too!"

"That's good."

"Their lives ran in parallel, before they ever met!"

"That's good."

Feifei looked down at her lap. "It is quite good," she said.

Now at last Linlin intuited. She leaned closer. The curve of Feifei's belly, the glow in her eyes. "How many months already? Did you tell Rong?"

"I didn't tell him yet." Feifei took from her purse a discount coupon that came with the pregnancy test. *Comfortable and painless! Nobody need ever know! Thirty percent off!* What do you advise, Big Sister? Of course I want a baby, but—"

"Aiya! The pollution in the environment," Linlin said. "Every day there's news about industrial chemicals turning up in water—in our milk, in our food, in our—"

"Yes, the environment—"

"Radioactivity!" She made a grand gesture, twinkling her fingers to indicate the dangerous radiation. "Who knows if anybody will ever be pregnant again?"

"You think we should have the baby, or we should not have the baby?"

Even as a little girl playing with dolls, Feifei had been the more maternal one.

"We'll have the baby, dearest sister."

It was a cold, snowless winter. The wind blew from the west. Linlin looked forward to becoming an aunt. The caricature of a Beijing auntie is a loud-mouthed know-it-all; she'd be up to taking on that role, now and again. She brought the mother-to-be nutritious pigeon eggs (though some so-called pigeon eggs, they say, are really just quail eggs with the spots artificially removed). She looked up advice online. Before going to sleep a pregnant woman should read a story with a happy ending. ("How come nobody writes that kind of story anymore?" Feifei asked.) Also she should avoid sex—according to Chinese websites, yet American ones permit it. Feifei decided to be American, in that regard.

To ease her back, Feifei would stand with her hands clutching her sides. "What kind of future will the child have?" she liked to speculate. "When the child is our age, China will be the richest, most powerful country on the planet!" Linlin didn't disagree—she was patriotic too—but there's no need to sound like you're addressing the Politburo. She thought she could detect Chen Rong's voice speaking through her sister, but perhaps it was the proud fetus expressing its opinion.

Now that she was free from George, Linlin indulged in carbohydrates, and Feifei was eating for two. From street vendors the sisters bought freshly roasted sweet potatoes that smelled like roses, and bags of chestnuts, scattering the husks like petals on the frost-sparkled curbs.

Linlin was working quite hard; she was part of the team putting together a bid for a major project in Qufu. Her office was a short subway ride from Houhai Lake, which was frozen over. Quite often she strolled there at lunchtime, and watched the chair-skaters and the laughing children spinning round. Once she went into a department store to check out baby clothing. On the escalator going down she passed a woman in a severe business suit going up, who hissed at her, "Watch out! We're keeping an eye on your associates!" The woman looked familiar—it was that Yang from the Hash, wasn't it? Well, there are bound to be business antagonisms; you can't read too much into it. Thoughtfully Linlin continued her descent past Men's Underwear. The packages of regular sizes had pictures of smirking male models—the kinds of models who sell everything. But for the XL and XXL, the models were white men. Nobody wants to resemble a paunchy Chinese, but you might identify with a substantial, successful Westerner. She wondered who these models were. She imagined a Yank or a Brit, fond of his beer and his pizza, brash, self-confident, proud to be on display in his underpants for all the world to see. It was almost a year since Linlin had set out along the ketchup route. It was strange not to have a foreign man to care about, to puzzle what was going through his head— but there were so many more hours in the day. She made a commitment to remain single until the birth.

Linlin was fond of Christmas—a festival that is just for fun, without any particular obligations to family or tradition. She volunteered to decorate the office tree, and she was on a stepladder tying a red star on the top when she got a call from a Hash acquaintance, Hugo.

"Hullo, Lin. Long time no chitchat!" He was BBC (British Born Chinese) and judging by his accent he might indeed be broadcasting on the World Service. "How's life been treating you?"

She replied coolly in Chinese, "I'm fine. And you, Hao?" She wondered what he wanted from her. He was handsome but had a reputation as a playboy.

"Yeah no. It's work-related, actually. I know, *bo-o-oring*." He switched to Chinese, the better to cut to the chase. "Do you want to do a job for me part-time?"

"Maybe," she said, echoing herself in both languages, "Maybe."

The fact was she didn't have enough to keep her occupied at work (the Qufu bid was out of her hands now, the responsibility of more senior management; she frittered at her computer, playing a game set in wartime Shanghai in which she is a spy outwitting the Japanese), though it was in her interest to give the illusion of being run off her feet.

Hugo was in PR, specializing in luxury products. He was offering a temporary position for the weeks leading up to Chinese New Year. He needed an attractive bilingual woman to go to expat bars and do promotions—*brand ambassador* is what it's called. "Sort of like going on a Hash, only you get paid for it." He told her how much she could expect to make in tips. In a single evening, she'd earn as much as she did in a week in her regular job.

"But I'm not—"

"Yeah, I know," he said. "It's just acting . . . *The quality of mercy is not strained.* . . . The girls who really are that kind of girl—by nature, born and bred—they can't hack it. It's just because it's who you're not it's who you can be."

This seemed to make a kind of sense in English.

"Oh go on, Lin," he said. And then in Chinese, "What are you afraid of?"

She didn't altogether trust him. The fronds of the plastic pine tree teased her with their un-smell. There were paper cutouts of snowflakes attached to the branches, and a silvery ball bobbed. She thought of the moon, and the rabbit who lives there, forever pounding the elixir of life. From on high she could see into cubicles where her coworkers were hard at it. Below her, old Mr. Collingwood was groaning, "My knees! My knees!" (It was climb-the-stairs Wednesday.) In business mode she said curtly, "I'll get back to you on it, Hugo."

An idea struck her. She descended from the tree and went in search of Zhijian, the go-to guy in technical support. She was aware of Facebook (she'd seen the movie), though it was banned in China. Zhijian showed her how to circumvent the firewall to access it. She clicked, clicked again, and here was George. It was less than three months since he'd last made love to her. He was married to some blonde named Cynthia. Googling led to their wedding announcement in the *Washington Post,* five years previously.

She returned to the tree, jabbed a switch, and the red star glowed.

Linlin emerged from her office building, and her brother-in-law was standing outside. It was a dull afternoon in January. He was wearing a sharply creased suit, and his eyeglass frames were in a fashionable style. His hair was cut short, making him look like an aged child.

He smiled and his teeth appeared too large for his mouth. "I'm on my way to an appointment," he said. "Can I drop you off somewhere?" He seemed to be exaggerating his speech defect, as if he took pride in it.

"I'm going to meet Feifei at the gym."

"Ah, of course."

A taxi was waiting. He got in next to her, and ordered the driver to head for the Second Ring Road. What did he want from her? He'd acquired an air of command, as if the pregnancy were proof of his manhood.

"How's Feifei?" Linlin asked.

"Everything is fine."

"The sonogram?" she said. "The blood tests?"

"My wife is excellent." He took off his glasses and breathed on them. "I have something to discuss with you."

The driver interrupted, and Rong gave the order to continue along the Ring Road until further notice.

He gave her an assessing stare. Objectively his manner

was not inappropriate; it was just that she had an image of him as a more reserved man. "You," he said, "and my wife." As if weighing the sisters in a balance, he shifted his cupped hands up and down. She wondered just for a moment if he were making a pass. Then he talked about his business relationship with Qin, "A financier with connections in high places, and with a beautiful wife too." And next, lowering his voice, in an indirect but unambiguous way, he spelled out what he wanted from her—followed by a disconcerting chuckle. How should she respond? She felt horror as well as a strange excitement. "It's what you were born to do, Lin." All she could say was that she needed time to reach a decision.

The taxi, having circled the heart of Beijing, returned past its starting point; she got off at the gym. As she took the elevator up, she wondered if she should mention this encounter to Feifei. But it wasn't the kind of thing her sister would want to know.

A month later, the snow had been plowed into roadside dunes, and the bar sign of MIND THE GAP in Nanluoguxiang was casting pink on patches of slush. Linlin and another brand ambassador were standing outside, dressed in purple-and and-gold kilts and matching low-cut blouses. Their shoes at least were practical. Against the cold, they had on a flesh-tone body stocking, fingerless gloves, and a rabbit-fur hat. They wore a sash with the name of the product, Old Mardi Gras

Whisky, and a tray jutting out between navel and bosom, loaded with many little plastic glasses. Hugo, smart in his college blazer, reassured Linlin. "If you have any questions, ask me or Tianhua. She's an old hand, aren't you, Tianhua?"

Tianhua grinned at her coworker. "Been there, done that." She had an Australian accent.

Hugo gave the spiel. "Let me tell you everything you need to know, ladies. Old Mardi Gras Whisky is concocted according to an ancient Scottish recipe in Chongqing. It's delicious, sophisticated, and it gets you drunk." He confided his marketing strategy. "We go for the expat and the hipster segments first. Then we conquer the mainstream. It's the trickle-down effect." He moved his finger and thumb down, as if indicating a drip from the eaves.

A crowd of curious bar-goers—mostly foreign—was assembling.

The winter air smelled of coal fumes.

Hugo raised a chopstick like a baton. He brought it down, and the whisky girls launched into song:

"I love Old Mardi Gras Whisky!

I love OMG!"

The girls repeated their jingle, and customers joined in, extending the final syllable.

Hugo coughed. "Beijing puts the OMG in smog! You heard it here first!"

A pretty bus girl scuttled out, bringing the liquor. More

customers appeared, coming out of the bar, and off the streets too; from every direction, men arrowed toward the brand ambassadors. "Plenty for everybody!" Hugo declared. "It's your lucky day!" Linlin saw foreigners and Chinese around her, heaped like a snow bank, then individuals coalesced out of the mass, lurching forward, their hands out like petitioners, the shine in their eyes matching the shine of the drink. She was vulnerable and dominant. The rule was, she had to pour the shots one by one, holding each glass close so it didn't get grabbed, and hand it to a customer. Sometimes too much came from the bottle, and a glass brimmed, its meniscus brilliant against the night.

"I love Old Mardi Gras Whisky!
I love OMG-G-G!"

The song recurred at intervals. No need for the whisky girls themselves to do it—the song was singing itself—as if an invisible finger kept tapping the replay button.

The bus girl, who was named Big Eyes, giggled. "Let's get the foreigners drunk!" She mimicked the sounds of American English (not real words, just nonsense syllables) and then British English.

"You're a little parrot," Linlin said.

"Parrots have got tiny eyes, and mine are big!"

Hugo had bead necklaces in the OMG colors, which he was trying to give out. But the men didn't want beads: they wanted whatever it was the whisky girls had to offer.

Hugo had a word with Tianhua, who in turn spoke to Linlin: "I'll go inside the bar," in English, and in Chinese, "A dragon in the tiger's cage," and back in English, "Are you okay without me, dear? You've got plenty of elbow room, and Hugo will look after you." In the headlights of a passing car, Linlin saw that Tianhua, though she made herself up to cover her blemishes, was well into middle age.

What was the worst that could happen? It was a simple job, really. Linlin learned how men drink in various ways. Some nuzzle with their eyes shut. Some lean forward and suck directly from the glass on the tray. Some squint, trying to watch the alcohol as it enters their bodies. About half the men said thank you. About half gave her a tip. (There was no correlation between the thanks and the tip.) White men let her pour for them, but Chinese men would take the empty glass in both hands and hold it up to be filled, which made her task more difficult.

How long did it last? Her life as a whisky girl was brief and eternal. Several times she felt her phone vibrate. Then Tianhua staggered out of the bar, her mascara smudged, and Hugo did a winding-down gesture. He cleared the glasses from the trays. With a shout of "Time! Gentlemen! Time!" he shooed away the last hopefuls, giving them a bead necklace as a consolation prize. He switched to a phony American accent: "That's all, folks! Elvis has left Beijing!"

A stray cat mewed, and she crouched to pet it. Just then

somebody in a panda suit drove by on an electric bicycle. For Linlin, tired and cold and dizzy from the whisky vapors, this coincidence (for in Chinese *Elvis* and *panda* are written literally as "cat king" and "cat bear") seemed a revelation of the workings of destiny. Big Eyes waved and called to the Panda, "When I grow up, I want to be you!" and did a little dance.

The door of the bar opened, and rock music blasted out. Hugo slid his arms around Tianhua. Honking taxis vied for a spot.

Drunken men spiraled on the slippery sidewalk, staring down. With the promotion now over, what were they supposed to do with their lives?

One of them came over. He sniggered, "Are you lean, Lin?" He mumbled an English idiom she didn't understand. Then, "Why not? You do it with all the others."

She couldn't go on like this. She retreated to the shadow of a boutique; inside its window, shoes were forever on the point of running off and dim mannequins in spring fashions lurked, and it seemed she was rising, observing the groupings from on high. She willed herself to be years in the future, her mind circling this moment . . .

She tugged up her kilt and pulled the phone from its pocket. She had a dozen messages from Feifei: *Please call, it's important.*

Once upon a time, two sisters were playing patty-cake, chanting a counting rhyme about picking orchids.

In a separate universe, Hugo's voice was summoning her in crisp English, "Come along, Lin! It's going-home time!" and Tianhua, tittering, was going, "Naughty, naughty!" and the drunk who'd propositioned her was coming to an arrangement with Big Eyes.

Linlin's life as a whisky girl was over, and she wasn't content to trudge up the corporate ladder. . . . But then there was Chen Rong's proposal. He'd appealed to her self-interest as well as her patriotism. In the taxi he'd disclosed that Qin was eager for inside tips on the Qufu bid, aiming to steer the contract to a Chinese company instead of a multinational. And this was no one-off; she'd supply regular information. She'd be rewarded for her determination and daring. She'd have enemies (what successful person doesn't?), but that would only add to the thrill of the game. What would her role be? To get in with powerful foreign men, to charm, to seduce, to turn their own power against them . . . "If you're going to consort with Westerners, you might as well get a substantial benefit from it." Now at last she understood where she belonged: in a network of people striving to help one another, standing or falling together—a family of sorts.

The phone rang; it was her sister. She pressed it to her ear, to hear above the music and the traffic. At the other end, a newborn girl was crying.

GIFT OF THE FOX SPIRIT

On Monday and Friday, his shirt is blue, on Tuesday and Saturday, yellow, on Thursday and Sunday, pink, and on Wednesday—ah, Wednesday is supposed to be his day off, but in practice he often has to work then, too, and since he can't wear the same color as on a day next to it (i.e., neither yellow nor pink) he's left with blue; the point being that if a shirt were the same color two days running, she might think he didn't change it, though of course he would anyway, out of respect, and she gives no sign of noticing his shirt rotation, perhaps regarding it as a natural cycle, as snow is succeeded by slush, then mud, then dust storms, then summer heat and flash floods, and soon it is pleasantly cool and once again leaves fall from the roadside trees. As another example of his professionalism, when he takes off his trousers at night, he lays them beneath the mattress: he and his wife sleep and dream and make love on top of them, and when he puts them on in the morning, they have a neat crease. Also, he avoids eating smelly foods in the car, for instance, pickles. When he drives her from her home near the Forbidden City to a favorite boutique or a restaurant where she is to meet up with other important wives, or to her husband's office, he is careful to avoid potholes. Sometimes she chooses to chat: "The traffic is slow today." "Yes, it is quite slow." There are things they have in common. Both were born in the Year of the Snake (she is twelve years older) and both are parents: his son is nine while her daughter is a sophomore at Tsinghua University. In their different ways, the chauffeur and the politician's wife are getting by.

Have they always played these roles? It might seem so, and in previous incarnations too: he has a recurrent dream in which he is a eunuch serving an empress. But even within this life he has lived other lives. He grew up in Daxing, on the outskirts of the city; as a child he helped feed the chickens and weed the watermelon patch. In his teens he was something of a rebel. . . . He was arrested for joyriding, and spent a scary six months in prison. . . . Then a matchmaking auntie introduced him to Meirong; they married, and her father got him a job as a taxi driver, working the night shift. Pimps and whores, the drunk and the drugged, actors and singers and people in reality shows . . . he had them all in his cab, and about once a week a customer would skip out without paying, and twice he was robbed at knifepoint. Beneath the paved streets of Beijing: the shifting desert.

Well, that's all ancient history. He's been a chauffeur for three years, long enough that the white gloves feel part of him. Everybody misses their first car—the old taxi drivers used to go all weepy when they remembered the Mian Di "yellow bugs"—but, if we're to be honest, cars, like most things, have gotten better over the years.

Meirong makes fun of his commitment to his job. She becomes the quizmaster on a TV special. "What sound does Mrs. Ximen make when she slurps her noodles? What brand of toilet paper does Mrs. Ximen use? When does Mrs. Ximen have her period?" He could answer all these questions; there is almost nothing a chauffeur does not know. But it's his wife whom he loves. He loves everything about her: her soft body, the silvery stretchmarks on her belly, her familiar smell . . . and when they're in bed together it's always their wedding night. He's always a bad boy, fresh out of jail; she's always his virginal bride, slender and innocent and shy.

In a way, though, she's right. He does have two women, just as Mrs. Ximen has two men. Meirong is a cleaner at the bus garage and works the swing shift. Weekday mornings she's still asleep when he drops Junjun off at school. Usually he's home early enough to put the boy to bed. (Otherwise Auntie Bo will do it.) By the time Meirong comes back, well after midnight, he's asleep, and she wakes him. He gets up and pees. Sometimes they make love. He drifts back to sleep, wrapped around her warm body.

Mrs. Ximen never asks about his wife, and she says little about her husband. (He has responsibilities for financial discipline, whatever that means.) But they do sometimes talk about their children. She'll praise her daughter, who is majoring in electrical engineering, then she might make a remark about his son's goldfish. About a year ago he took Junjun to a secondhand car market as a treat, and like a vision a beautiful woman appeared. She was tall and wearing a long red coat with a smudgy fur collar, and she was clattering along on high heels. She was crying; her eyes were all in a mess. She put something small and shiny in Junjun's hand, and she strode away so fast nobody could follow her. "Who is she, Daddy? Is she your friend?" "I don't know, Junjun." It was mysterious. If you believed in fox spirits, you might think she was one of those. The gift turned out to be a transparent bag and inside it there was water and a fish. At first, he thought the fish was for eating, but of course you don't eat a fish that fancy—it had flouncy bits, like a butterfly or a party hat. Junjun looked it up on the internet: it was a kind of goldfish called a Shubunkin, and its name was Bubbles. They kept it in a bowl in the TV room. All day long it swam round and round its pagoda. Well, he didn't tell Mrs. Ximen the whole story, but he did say that his son had this pet, and she said her daughter once had a Tibetan mastiff till her husband gave it away to his business associate. Now, one night in winter Meirong came home late as usual. "Get up, old hubby." She led him into the TV room, and there was Bubbles, belly-up on the surface, dead as can be. Who knows why? Who knows why it was their fate to have the pet in the first place? In the morning, he told the boy that the fox spirit had returned and taken Bubbles away with her. The boy was too old to believe the story, but he didn't contradict his father. Surely he understood. And Meirong said Bubbles was such a good fish, he'd be reincarnated as a shark or a whale. When he went to work he took the fish with him wrapped in newspaper, and in Ritan Park the gardeners were burning a heap of prunings, and he put the fish on the fire. But he never told Mrs. Ximen about the death. He's careful not to say anything that might upset her. She's delicate in her way, not half as tough as Junjun. So even now, in the summer, when she asks, "How's your Junjun? How's Bubbles?" he replies, "They're doing very nicely, thank you."

The Geely GE is a special car, suitable for Mrs. Ximen. It's red and elegant and it has only one grand seat at the back. Her favorite car music is Johann Sebastian Bach. He's come to appreciate it; its rhythms go along with the ever-flowing traffic. Nothing is ever lost; nothing is without consequences; whatever you think you've put behind you, for good or ill it'll come back again. Sometimes after he's dropped her off he rolls down the windows and cranks the volume up, blasting Bach into the city. Mr. Ximen has an Audi 12 and two chauffeurs who take turns, so he's always got somebody to drive him, day or night. Mr. and Mrs. Ximen live quite separate lives; it's not often that the Geely is parked next to the Audi, and he gets to have a smoke with one of the other chauffeurs, who are in fact brothers and soccer fans. Once, when Beijing Guo'an was up against Shanghai Shenhua, all three chauffeurs were watching on TV in a dumpling shop, and when the brothers' team scored the decisive goal—a brilliant header from a free kick—they launched into a cheer routine, complete with thumbs-up gesture and clapping, and he joined in too. *Guo'an! Let's go!* Six fists punched high in the air.

Mr. Ximen has a mustache, oddly enough. He wonders if Mrs. Ximen likes it. Since Mrs. Ximen doesn't smoke, he can't do it in or next to the Geely—which is a good thing, really; it helps him cut back. But Mr. Ximen puffs away like a chimney; he lets his chauffeurs have as many of his as they want. Zhongnanhai, that's the brand. When he enjoys a Zhongnanhai passed on by a brother, he feels the important smoke entering his lungs, Mr. Ximen's breath inside him.

Being a chauffeur may not be the most prestigious of jobs, but if a city is owned by anybody, it's by its drivers. He pities the pedestrians crawling like ants, the limited cyclists, and even the car owners at the back, occupied with laptop and documents, in the autumn of their tinted windows. He has witnessed extraordinary things, for example location shoots. Once he saw a street transformed with signs in English— Beijing standing in for New York. They were filming a chase scene. A stretch limo slammed into a police car, and the stuntman driver rolled out.

And there is a fourth chauffeur—though he's never met

him personally; he only knows what the brothers have passed on. He's from Shanghai, of all places. He smokes mentholated (whoever heard of a chauffeur smoking mentholated?) and is fond of sunflower seeds. He drives Mr. Ximen's mistress. That's really all he's been told about the man. He pictures him doing the trick that sunflower seed addicts are so skilled at: putting the seed in the mouth, and cracking the shell between the front teeth and spitting it out. He doesn't know a thing about the mistress—not her name or what she looks like. She'd be young and beautiful, of course, with quite large breasts and hips. She might be from Shanghai, like her chauffeur. He doesn't suppose she smokes mentholated. He sees an Audi 12 parked in a quiet country lane, a naked woman on the back seat. She's eating sunflower seeds. The husks fall, and gather on her belly. He takes off his white gloves and puts his arms around her, and kisses her, and she passes a seed into his mouth.

One day in June, Mrs. Ximen doesn't need him for a few hours—she's having French pastries with some of her wives—so he decides on a whim to head over to the bus garage and surprise Meirong. He gets on the Fourth Ring Road, and exits toward Shijingshan, and as he gets nearer he worries that he might get her into trouble. She's not supposed to have family around while she's working. So he decides he'll just say hello and leave it at that. He parks opposite her garage. There she is, in coveralls—she looks quite sexy in them—with a big hose in her hand, blasting mud off the asphalt. For some reason he thinks of a zoo-keeper washing down an elephant. He makes a call on his cell. Meirong turns off the hose. "Yes?" she says into her cell. He says, "I'll be a little late this evening. Auntie Bo will fetch Junjun from school." "Okay."

When he was about nineteen he was at an illegal dance party in a warehouse. It was the kind of music called punk. He didn't know much about it, but somebody had given him an invitation. He jumped up and down next to two beautiful girls. He showed them the snake tattoo on his arm. The older girl had drawn a monkey on her shoulder with ballpoint, and the younger had quite a realistic rooster. The three of them banged heads together, and afterward he kissed them in the parking lot, his ears ringing. The band changed names a few times, and eventually became SUV Flu, which is big on the Beijing punk circuit, and he was at their first gig! The lead vocalist was dressed as a panda, and the drummer banged away at a terra-cotta warrior. He saw them before they were famous! If somebody had told him back then that one day he'd desire nothing more than to be a husband and father and hold down a regular job, he'd never have believed it.

He and Junjun like watching crime shows on TV. At the beginning: a dead body. The detective follows the leads and works out whodunnit. There's often a chauffeur in the show, a nonspeaking part. Everybody else is just pretending, but the actor playing the chauffeur really does drive a car, so in a way he's the only real person.

Time to head back. He picks up Mrs. Ximen at the Hurong French Pastry Shop. She has a bruise over her cheekbone, not large. Probably she's had it for quite a while, but now he notices it.

A few weeks later, they have a conversation about space exploration. (It stays in his mind, because it's on the same day that Meirong brings home the newspaper from the bus garage.) They're driving along Chang'an Avenue, and it's sunset, and the crows are swaying on the poplars, and she's sneezing on account of her allergies, and she says that her daughter is applying for an internship in the space program.

"She's going to be an astronaut?"

"She'll help design a communications satellite."

"Maybe she'll be an astronaut too? Maybe she'll be the first Chinese person on the moon?"

"Did your Junjun learn about space, in school?"

"He built a rocket ship." The words come out of their own accord. He didn't intend to make so bold a claim. "The whole class together, they made it from . . . an icicle radish!" He laughs. He can see it as clearly as if he made it with his own hands—a long one, with hairy sprouts at the base, like exhaust gases, and a little national flag pinned to its side.

Mrs. Ximen—who never normally laughs—does so. "Let's

fly away in a radish!" The fantasy strikes him as inappropriate, even silly, but it cannot be silly if Mrs. Ximen approves of it, in this world where there is only the two of them.

That night, Meirong pulls his ear till he wakes and she shows him the newspaper—not even a whole one, just a few pages. It was left behind on a bus. It's one of those shadowy publications, the kind that come out for a few months till the authorities shut them down, and they reappear under a different name. It's called *The Real China Times*, and seems to be a pirated copy of a Hong Kong newspaper. "Look! Look! It's your Ximen family." The headline is POLITICIAN NUR-TURES YOUNG TALENT. There's a photograph of Mr. Ximen standing next to a pretty woman. He's seeking to appoint her to a position as Senior Investigator of Financial Irregularities, at an annual salary of two hundred thousand yuan. Meirong reads out the conclusion: "We congratulate Mr. Ximen on his ability to spot fantastic talent. We're sure Little Meixin is worth every fen of her very attractive salary plus perfectly shaped expenses."

"What's it mean?" he says sleepily.

"You've got to read between the lines, old hubby! They're saying Mr. Ximen is paying his mistress with government money."

He stares into the photograph. He pictures this Yang Meixin eating sunflower seeds. "It's nonsense," he says. "Nobody reads this kind of trash anyway."

The following morning he goes to a cyber café. (Junjun taught him some tricks for using a search engine.) He finds the story copied on many sites. And there are further accusations: that the woman tried to extort money from a leading banker named Qin, threatening to make a false charge against him unless he paid up. You can't believe the internet. People are always saying bad things about politicians. People even say bad things about Mao, and he was born in the Year of the Snake.

Mrs. Ximen must know about this scandal. Probably she learned it was about to break days ago, or weeks. He reckons she was a looker herself when she was young; her beauty took her where she is today. Surely Mr. Ximen was in love with her once; perhaps he still does love her, in his way.

The following day she's wearing a new pair of shoes, the way she does when she's unhappy. "How's Junjun?" she says mechanically, her voice swelling behind the back of his head. "How's Bubbles?"

"Junjun's fine." He waits, gathering power from the silence. He overtakes a file of electric bikes, then slows to let a van go past. "The fish is dead."

"Oh no! How awful! Not Bubbles!" Her sadness may be real but seems fake. From her reaction, you'd think the death of a goldfish is comparable to an earthquake and a tsunami and a ruptured nuclear reactor, disaster on disaster on disaster. "When did this happen? Did it happen this morning?"

"This morning, yes," he says, taking the cue.

"And you went straight out and bought a replacement?"

"I did," he says, realizing this is what he should have done, months ago. Another Shubunkin for Junjun, or a different fish? Maybe a different pet? Might his son prefer a hamster, or even a puppy?

"What do you call the new goldfish?" she asks.

"Ah . . . Feilin," he says, plucking the name from the air—recalling the punk girls. He liked Linlin, the one with the monkey. He liked her friend, Feifei too; it was difficult to decide. The girls were young, lying about their age. They said they were sisters, probably lying about that as well. Anyway they were too posh for him; it never would have worked out. It was to impress the girls that he stole the Buick Regal, and he made love to them in the back of it, and all his troubles began.

She says, "My husband and I, we're taking a break for a few weeks . . . the countryside . . . our little place near Badaling . . ."

"When?"

"Tomorrow. We're leaving tomorrow."

"But—"

"Of course, you'll receive your full salary, while we're away."

In the rearview mirror her expression is unrevealing. Why won't she open up to him? Why won't she share her fear? That Mr. Ximen will be demoted; he'll resign; he'll be banged up in a cell smaller than his Audi. That Mrs. Ximen will no longer be driven around in her glamorous automobile with shag carpeting and European music.

In another world, he'd park, whether she requests him to or not. He'd get out and open the door at the back, and he'd join her inside, the two of them on that one grand red seat. She'd be crying and he'd cry too: politician's wife and chauffeur, empress and eunuch, would melt into each other.

The lights change.

A bark of the horn. To the accompaniment of the "Well-Tempered Clavier" he steps on the accelerator and charges ahead of the pack. The car rumbles across a sewer cover and bounces over a pothole. If he loses his job, somebody's going to pay him off. Mr. Ximen can compensate him, or that Yang woman might have some money, or Kong can do him a favor, or. . . . They'll give him what he's entitled to nicely, or if not. . . . It's not only rich people who've got connections. He's got connections, too, through the people he met as a taxi driver, and from his time in jail. Anybody who crosses him, they'll get what they deserve.

"Do you like my shirt?" he asks Mrs. Ximen. "Today is Friday and my shirt is blue."

When he gets back home in midafternoon, his wife is still there, eating her breakfast porridge.

"I met a woman at the hairdresser," she says, before he

can speak. "She and her husband own a successful plumbing business, and they're expecting a baby. She used to be a maid in California, until she was deported. She worked for a rich lawyer who drove his own car."

"Well, he can't have been very rich then."

"He was a millionaire. He had plenty of servants—a gardener, a housekeeper . . . he even had somebody who came just to clean his pool—but he drove himself."

"A hobby?"

"The millionaire was overseas Chinese, but he behaved like an American."

"So what did his chauffeur do?"

"Aren't you listening, old hubby? He didn't have a chauffeur."

"What? None at all?"

She holds him a while, her hands over his ears so he hears noises like distant traffic; then, "Off to the bus garage!"

She walks out into the summer heat.

He drives to Junjun's school. He's early; the children are still in class. He circles the block, looking for parking, and thinks how much of his life has been spent in that patient, inquisitive creep. The radio plays a medley of hits from when he was his son's age.

Soon enough Junjun emerges. His son announces for the benefit of the other boys, "My daddy's got the amazingest car in China!"

"Hop in," he says, getting out and ushering in his son, the way he would his employer.

Junjun climbs in and perches on the red throne at the back, his hands on the chair-arms, as if about to swing forward. He tucks his feet under his bottom, to grow a little taller. He babbles a story they learned in school, about Emperor Qin who had a magic needle that made the sun stand still, and a whip that moved mountains . . .

A glance at the wing mirror. "There's something I need to tell you."

"When I grow up, I want a Geely just like this!"

They drive to a small family restaurant. They get meat buns and fermented mung bean juice, to go. Father and son shelter in the air-conditioned car and eat with noisy abandon. Afterward the smell lingers, the ghost-meal continuing, song dissolving into song.

They get out and the remains go in the trash.

"Teach me to drive, Daddy!"

A mass of black cloud is advancing from the horizon. He pats his pockets and finds a single, precious, wrinkled cigarette. He cups it in both hands, against the wind.

"Can I have a drag, Daddy?"

He brings the cigarette to his son's mouth.

The boy coughs valiantly. "I won't tell Mama," he promises.

He tries to confide in a way his son will understand, "Sometimes a car is like a fish . . ." and Junjun is insisting,

"Daddy! Teach me to drive!" and there is no time for confession or advice because . . . behind them: a sliding shadow—footsteps—a car door slamming. . . . A figure, a teenager, by the look of him, is hunched in the driver's seat of the Geely.

The man yells.

The engine starts up and the car screeches from the curb. It stalls, lurches, speeds away.

He shakes his fists in the air. He dances with rage. "Dog-fucked! Plague god! Son of a rabbit!" He curses the teenager, curses his parents, curses his ancestors to the eighteenth generation. It's been years since he let his anger rip. He feels alive.

A dazzling whiteness rises beneath the storm cloud, like the ash of a sacrifice. A distant hiss, coming closer. Then the whole sky turns an electric gray..

The absence of the Geely counts, for now, as a kind of solution.

There's a taxi parked across the road. An overweight driver is standing next to it, yawning. Junjun runs over.

"Chase that car!"

"I'm not chasing any car," the driver says. "I'm on my break."

"We've got to catch the bad guy!"

"What do you think this is? The movies?"

Heavy raindrops begin to fall.

Junjun jumps into the driver's seat.

"Hey you! Get out of there!" The indignant taxi driver flaps his arms.

"Help me, Daddy!"

He climbs in next to his son. They can see—in the distance, stuck at the lights—the Geely.

"After him!" they shout. The one turns the key; the other releases the brakes. They grip the wheel between them. The man wants what the boy wants.

A bolt of lightning eternalizes the city.

Thunder comes. The taxi swims into traffic . . . The Geely blurs . . . becomes tantalizingly clear . . . again a blur. . . . And the chase continues, in ever slower motion, as glowing rain encases their lives and windshield wipers row through the drowned world.

YEAR OF THE PANDA

She sells her body to save her mother's life. If they made her the star of a reality show, that would be the tagline. The series would end with the mother's funeral; or else with a wedding: the heroine marries a perfect man, and the mother is magically restored to health. She breathes in and out, holding her smile, as she struts along the catwalk, which is not really a catwalk—just a zone indicated with masking tape on the hardwood floor of a loft in a warehouse in northeast Beijing.

The dress feels tight in places, gripping and releasing her as she moves. She knows she looks good in it; more to the point, it looks good on her.

The call was unexpected. She was at home, scrubbing algae off an aquarium ornament in the shape of a pagoda. An extended grunt, then, "Hey! It's me."

"Who are you?"

"It's me. Guoqing. I need you."

"Who?"

"No bullshit. Remember me?" The whiny voice is distinctive.

"Ah, I remember you, Guoqing. You should go through my agent."

"Fuck your agent! What's your agent ever done for you?"

Actually her agent has done a great deal for her, though little recently. She's twenty-five—which, in model-years, is equivalent to seventy-five in human years. Guoqing hired her a few times, a while back. She's aware of his reputation as an independent designer, innovative, a freelancer for fashion houses. He goes by just his personal name, as if he had no family, as if like the Monkey King he was born from a stone.

"Listen," he said. "I want *you*. I don't want some skinny teenager who looks fabulous but has no idea how to play the game. I don't care about your wrinkles. I don't care if you've put on weight around the hips. I know you know how to make my clothing look like a million dollars."

"You sure know how to flatter a girl."

"I'll pay you the same I paid you when you were twenty-one."

If her agent caught word of this, he might drop her. But this was an opportunity she couldn't afford to pass up. Guoqing explained: he has a new line coming out. He was planning to give an ultra-private showing—just a single dress presented to a few select buyers. A teaser. Don't show everything at once. Show enough to hook them, and they'll come back for more.

And here she is, on the catwalk that is not really a catwalk, in an industrial building out beyond the Fifth Ring Road. She's done this so often before. Doing it again is like going back to a place you used to live in as a child. It's strange.

Normally there'd be applause, music, loud conversation. But there's almost silence here, apart from the muted roar of the fan-heater and a few wintry coughs. No camera flashes, either. Cameras and phones are banned. Nobody is going to rip off Guoqing's design and bring a copy to market before the real thing comes out.

She turns her head as she advances, taking in the scene. Guoqing in a double-breasted tweed suit and brilliant shoes. Eight buyers on folding chairs, leaning forward. Big windows with gray clouds beyond. She concentrates on her task . . . the audience vanishes, the building itself vanishes, all that exists is herself walking along this strip of wood raised high in the sky.

The designer holds up his hand. That's it.

Decent applause, after all.

He shoos her away to the changing room. Which is not a real changing room, either—just a corner of the loft, screened off with a sheet suspended from a rope.

She asked the doctor about the options; her mother was having dialysis. He was quite young, with a mole at the corner of his mouth that she couldn't help focusing on.

"A kidney transplant?" the doctor said, leaning closer than was necessary. "Is that what you're thinking of? Well, you could donate one of yours, or find a peasant to sell his. The operation's not cheap, either way. Anyway, I don't recommend it. Your mother's got problems with her heart and her lungs, and there's her liver too. . . . Even if you spent a million yuan on her health care, we can't do miracles."

Dialysis takes time. It's a slow process, the cleansing of the blood, the impurities being filtered out of it. Meanwhile she stays in the waiting area. She knows it all too well. There's a food concession that sells soy milk, another for skewered meat. There's a counter to buy traditional herbal medicine, and a counter for modern medicine. There's a Mickey Mouse and a qilin and a dragon big enough for a child to sit on; if a parent drops a coin in the slot, a mythical creature rocks to and fro and an electronic jingle plays.

In this changing room that is not a changing room, the only furnishing is a plastic chair; she left her street clothes and her handbag on it. They're not here now. Somebody— Guoqing, presumably—moved her belongings. He's so inconsiderate. They're all inconsiderate. She's had it up to here with the world of fashion. It's like a landlord exploiting the peasants. She can't march out and ask for her things. She can't come out at all, until the buyers have left. It's her job, now, to be unseen and unheard.

She hears his voice through the sheet. "Give me the dress!"

"Guoqing, where are my—?"

"Give me the dress now. I need it to show the clients."

"Where are—?"

"Give me the fucking dress! I put your shit in the closet for safekeeping."

She strips off the dress. She has nothing on underneath. She pushes the dress over the top of the sheet, and it is instantly yanked away.

She is alone, naked, apart from her high heels. Which should feel weird, but it seems familiar. Like a medical examination, she thinks.

She's spent too much of her life visiting hospitals. Her father died of cancer when she was twelve. He lagged pipes, for a living. If it hadn't been for the Cultural Revolution he'd have gone to university. If he'd survived, and encouraged her in school, perhaps she'd have a proper education herself. The only gift she has from him is his genes: the height and bone structure, the shape of the eyes.

White noise. The blast of the fan heater seems to conceal a musical beat. An overlay of several voices, one of them Guoqing's, which she can't quite disentangle. Fashion talk? A negotiation? An argument?

The house she grew up in, the entire neighborhood, was demolished the year after her father died. She and her mother were obliged to move to an anonymous apartment building in Fengtai. More than to her daughter, her mother speaks to the goldfish; she whispers *I love you* into the tank.

The voices can no longer be heard.

The fan heater also has stopped; the absence of that noise is eerie.

She calls out, "Guoqing?"

Louder, "Guoqing? Where are you?"

She snatches at the sheet, pulling it down. She drapes it over her body.

Nobody and nothing is here. The entire loft is empty. There is no indication that a fashion show just took place; even the masking tape has been pulled from the floor.

She is stranded, all but naked, on the fifth floor of a warehouse. She has no phone, no money. She looks out at the low sky. Dirty snow on roofs and on the streets.

She howls.

Guoqing, that bastard! Why did he do it? What was his scheme? And then: How can I be sure it was him? A voice, sounding something like his, called to her, asked for the dress. Perhaps it was one of the buyers, imitating Guoqing's voice? Yes, one of the buyers stole the dress, and stole her belongings, too, so she can't escape and raise the alarm!

A saying comes to mind, the call-and-response greeting of the Young Pioneers. *Are you prepared? . . . Always be prepared!* Instinctively she raises her right hand in the Pioneer salute, and lets the useless sheet fall. The heater is no longer on; the loft will soon get cold. She flicks a light switch, to no effect. The electricity is not working.

She kicks off her painful shoes.

The emptiness of the place is almost absolute, a desolation. She roams the confines, not troubling to avoid splinters. In one corner there is a life-size stuffed panda, its face to the wall like a naughty child. On the opposite wall, a closet. She tugs the door. Several plastic coat hangers jostle on a rail. Her street-clothing? Her handbag? No. Of all things, a terra-cotta warrior. It gazes out at her from the dimness, like a child playing eluding-the-cat, its head at the level of her breasts.

She guesses this space is used for photo shoots. The panda and the warrior—these would be props, left behind.

She holds the panda in her arms. It is light.

The warrior is grimy. She grips it around the shoulders, as if wrestling with it. It is heavier than it looks, and seems to be made of plaster.

The panda, again. A zip at the back. As she undoes it, nuggets of Styrofoam fall out. She can't help stepping on them; they squeak under her soles like dry, synthetic mice.

The panda is actually a costume, she realizes. She pours out its stuffing. The paws and head are attached with Velcro, and she detaches them. She enters it. She manages to pull up the zipper. Now she puts the head back on; she can see well enough through the eyeholes. The paws, finally. She notices a plastic camellia abandoned on the floor of the closet, and she winds the stem around the neck, accessorizing her outfit.

She presses the elevator button; no light goes on.

In the panda suit, carrying the plaster warrior, she walks down the emergency stairs, all five flights.

At the bottom: a fire exit. She tries to push the bar. Locked.

A small window next to it, not big enough to squirm through.

Using the warrior as a battering ram, she attacks the window.

The warrior's head dissolves into shards of plaster and dust, revealing a rusted steel armature within. The pane is intact.

Harder this time, yelling as if performing a martial art, she smashes the armature into the window frame, and at last the glass shatters. An icy gust. She reaches through the gap and gropes for a knob, which she succeeds in turning.

She's in a parking lot. Slush on the ground. A yellow patch where a dog or pedestrian pissed. A few cars and vans, but no human within sight. On the far side of the lot, traffic speeds by. She knows roughly where she is. (She came by taxi.) She's in an industrial area many kilometers from the center. She can't walk far in her costume. And where would she go anyway? She can't go home like this. (Those nosy old biddies on the Residents Committee—they'd interrogate her before letting her in. There'd be no end of gossip.) She can't go to the police. Then she thinks of one person in the whole of Beijing who might be able and willing to help her.

Among the vans and trucks and pickups in the lot, there's an electric bicycle. She gets on it. It starts up. She doesn't know how much juice the battery's got, but there's no alternative. It will take her as far as it will take her.

Making her way along less busy roads, she heads toward the center. Some honks and stares, but no more than she gets walking down the street on any normal day. Maybe in some other city a panda on a bicycle would be a marvel; the traffic would halt and a wide-eyed crowd would shout and snap photos; it would become an excuse for a mini-carnival, with food vendors and skipping children and a skateboarder performing twisty jumps and men singing a patriotic song in chorus and elderly women waltzing with each other . . . people would project their hopes and fears on it, as on an Immortal. But Beijingers temper curiosity with blaséness: we've seen it all before.

A mother is laden with shopping. A little girl tugs the mother's arm. "Look! Look!" The mother drags the child onward and does not look.

A seeing-eye dog woofs at her.

Laborers shoveling snow pay her no attention.

Bears in general are taken to be masculine. That's the thing about being male, even a male panda: you can go about in public in relative anonymity.

At the same time as she's gliding through the city on her electric bicycle, she feels that she's outside herself, viewing the image from afar. The present is a kind of memory. She's a fan of a TV series in which the hero goes back in time to the reign of Emperor Qin Shihuang, who buried Confucian scholars alive and burned *The Book of Songs*. (Yet in school she was taught that the Emperor was the glorious unifier of China.) The time traveler seeks to change history, but his intervention brings about the very harm he's trying to prevent.

She follows the signs for the Haidian District, going west. . . . Ah, the route is familiar, though it's almost a year since she last came here. Yes, the dumpling place; yes, the barber shop (judging by the décor, it's now operating as a brothel); there's a demolition site where there used to be a car showroom. . . . She slows and steers onto the sidewalk, swerving to avoid a snowdrift. And there, where you wouldn't expect it, a surviving old-fashioned house, with an arch in front and traditional eaves. (The neighboring houses were knocked down years ago.) She walks around the back to a modern addition with French windows. A desk; behind it a man is typing at a computer, his fingers pausing then skittering across the keyboard, like a cat pouncing on a mouse.

She raps at the glass. "Help me! Help me, Mr. Kong! I'm so sorry to inconvenience you!"

The man gets up, waddles over, and, grinning, lets the stranger in.

"Friend or foe?" he says. "You're welcome, either way!"

She tells him who she is.

"Ah, Lan," he says. "What an unexpected pleasure! You look gorgeous in the costume. But you look gorgeous in everything."

Soon, with her head and paws off, the panda is on the couch, drinking a gin and tonic and telling her story. The man, short and fat as Buddha, huddles on the swivel chair with his feet off the ground, inhaling his gin, and he listens intently.

Kong is a journalist, with a reputation for being a muckraker. He edits *The Real China Times*, a scandal sheet that pretends to be published in Hong Kong. He's famous also for his salons. He invites an extraordinary mix of people: artists and writers and political activists, even foreigners sometimes, and of course a sprinkling of beautiful women. The name he goes by is a pen name, and though he passes for a Beijinger he actually came to the capital as a young man, and never left. She remembers Kong once boasting about having exposed a corrupt politician, who sent him death threats. Somebody asked Kong if he was scared, and he snorted, "If the bastard meant to kill me, I'd be dead already." She used to go there every month, before her mother became sick. It was an education for her, the nearest she got to attending university.

A carpet is draped over the couch. She resists the urge to stretch out on it while she talks.

He hardly questions or comments, tugging an earlobe from time to time.

When she comes to the part about being naked in the warehouse, he smiles. She's aware of what he's visualizing, and she's aware that he's aware that she's aware. She's striking rather than pretty—tall with a square jaw—so she was hit on by drunken intellectuals at his salons more rarely than some of the other models. Kong himself made passes at her every time—at all the beautiful women, but especially at her. The fact that they'd make such an absurd couple—the dwarfish man and the statuesque woman—she guesses this is part of the attraction, for him. *The princess kisses a toad . . .* but that's a European fairy tale. In Chinese legends, beautiful women are either paragons who end up committing suicide, or they are courtesans who bring about the fall of a kingdom.

She tells him her theory that one of the buyers stole the dress.

He laughs. A slow, deep, intentional chuckle.

She's shocked. How can he make a joke of her suffering? She stammers, "I could have died in there!"

He laughs again, sneering, relishing the moment.

"Ah, you're so innocent, Lan! Such a sweet, innocent girl!"

"I could have frozen to death!"

"I'll tell you what really happened, Little Lan. A buyer didn't steal the dress. You did!"

"What are you saying?!"

"That's what Guoqing wants people to believe." In his intensity, he almost falls off the swivel chair; he looks like one of those toys which when knocked over rights itself. "Don't you get it, my darling Lan? Guoqing set you up!

You're the patsy, the fall guy! He's going to sell his dress to some fashion house, and at the same time he's going to steal it from himself."

"I don't understand."

"He's going to sell it twice. First to the company he has an official contract with, and second unofficially to another company who'll produce a pirated version. And when the first company finds out, he'll need somebody to blame. 'Oh no, it wasn't me who pirated myself, it was that thieving model, Lan.'"

"But surely—"

"Why do you think he chose you? Why didn't he hire a model through an agency?"

"He was trying to save the commission."

"Guoqing doesn't care about saving a few yuan! He chose you just because everybody knows you're on the way out and you've got a sick mother—exactly the kind of model who'd be tempted to steal."

"What are you saying?"

"You mean, how many years will you spend in jail?"

She shivers in her warm costume. Kong mixes her another gin and tonic, and pushes it into her hand. He taps his own glass on the table.

"You've come to the right fellow, Little Panda. This is exactly the kind of injustice I love to write about."

"Oh, please—"

"Ah, don't worry. I won't splash the story of your disgrace all over the gutter press. I'll find a way to save your neck."

She gulps the gin—a drink whose taste she dislikes—and begins to hope. She has faith in Kong's powers.

And what will he expect in return? If sex, she'll have to consent, at least to some degree. What else does she have to offer? There are only certain futures for a model on the brink of retirement. Acting, PR work . . . and marriage, ideally. Or darker prospects. Her friend, Ying, once she was on the cover of Taiwan *Vogue,* and now she's the mistress of a tiling tycoon from Ningbo. Ying suggested she could fix Lan up with her lover's business partner. Lan didn't accept the offer, but she didn't exactly say no either. Ying will make the suggestion again, and how will Lan answer? She could live a luxurious lifestyle, and her mother would receive the best care. Ying said: "It's better to have sex with an ugly man. That way, there's no confusion."

Kong opens a drawer and takes out a bulky, professional camera.

He explains that she'll have to get fully suited up again, and they'll go outside and he'll take photos of her on the bicycle. "I'll plant a story in one of the magazines—a short piece, the kind we call a 'tofu cube'—how you were hired to do publicity at the opening of a shopping mall, dressed as a panda, and because it was so cold you wore the panda suit on the way home. We'll need some pics of you in full costume, and some with the head off, so you can be recognized."

"But if Guoqing—"

"I'll change the clock on the camera, to give you an alibi. You can't have been the model in the warehouse. You were somewhere else at the time. It'll be Guoqing's word against the evidence of the pics. The camera doesn't lie!"

"But—"

"In English they call this a 'human interest story.' A kind of fiction, really." He translates the idiom into Chinese and smiles in a less obnoxious way. "If pandas published newspapers, they'd call it a 'panda interest story.'"

He puts on a tall fur hat and a down coat covered with a deep blue material, giving him the air of a Qing Dynasty court official. They head out into the cold, and he leads her to a crossroads a short distance away.

She poses on the bicycle—many shots from many different angles. This at least she knows how to do. She attracts more attention from passersby now than she did when she was on her own. The fact of the camera: this gives the image resonance, makes it stand outside its own moment.

A passing trucker rolls down his window and hails her as Jingjing— the panda mascot in the Olympics. "One world, one games!" he chants the slogan.

There was something on the internet about how scientists are observing pandas in the wild; to conceal themselves, the scientists themselves dress as pandas. She visualizes panda-men among the bamboo. . . . And the scene dissolves into her mother in bed, the varicose veins on her legs like English writing.

She rides slowly, away from Kong and toward him along the street—distantly trailed by several small boys and a mutt.

He takes more pictures of her than anybody could possibly want.

Then back to his place.

There's a chest at the bottom of the stairwell where he keeps items left behind by guests at his salons. He burrows in the chest like a badger and tosses out items of apparel. Sweatpants and a fisherman's jersey, a pair of sneakers—things she can fit into and look normal enough.

She changes in the bathroom. She ceases being a panda. One day, conceivably, she'll think of this adventure with nostalgia. A grain of Styrofoam bobs in the toilet. She rests the camellia on the ledge above the sink. Between outfits, naked, she regards herself in the mirror. If she doesn't look too carefully, her body is still perfect.

She returns to the writing room.

He phones for a cab.

There are words that men say when they want you; he offers only his detached smile.

Even to the last, she expects that he'll take her in his arms and press his lips on hers. The very idea makes her shudder. But he never does.

He pays the driver in advance and sends her away, back toward her dying mother and the goldfish.

The radio is on in the cab—the latest hit from SUV Flu, its raucous punk beat accompanying visuals of the city.

As she is whisked through the night streets of Beijing— silhouettes of roadside heaps of cabbage that will feed the poor through the winter, melding with dark, dirty snow-drifts—she understands that Kong's satisfaction was in his laughter. He sneered at her weakness even as he took pity on her. And she knows that things will become harder before they become easier, but she will have the memory of the short, fat man laughing at her, to sustain her through the suffering that lies ahead.

SCRATCHING THE HEAD OF
CHAIRMAN MAO

"Don't you get it?" Crow laughs. "The guy saw the barber pole, and he thought we're a whorehouse! He thought Master Cao was a pimp! He was from out of town, but you'd think he could tell the difference! If he wants that kind of 'barbershop,' he can go out along the Ring Road. There are plenty of places there, with plenty of girls, open all night long!"

"So did he get his hair cut?"

"That was the funny thing. He sat down, and I gave him a quick trim. I guess he thought he might as well go through with it, since he was here anyway. I shaped him along the sides, and I gave him a scalp massage too."

It's after dark, and Crow is the only barber left in the place. His girlfriend, Big Eyes, has dropped in, as she often does after she's finished at the boutique. He sweeps up the fallen hair and dumps it in the recycling bin.

"Who's your other girlfriend?" Big Eyes says.

"What other girlfriend?"

"What's she got that I haven't got?"

"Ah, you're all I can handle, Big Eyes."

She points to a lump of Styrofoam the size of an ostrich egg, with a nylon wig on top. Eyes and mouth are crudely inked on the "face." It's balanced on an improvised torso, a sweatshirt stuffed with cardboard. *"Adorable,"* she says—her favorite, multipurpose adjective.

"Oh that," he says. "We use it for practicing our new hairstyles."

"Who's prettier, Crow? Me or her?"

"The Styrofoam is prettier, ha ha!"

"That's not nice."

"We think of it as a man, actually. Our nickname for it is Da Shan." More generously he says, "I guess it could be a girl instead, I mean, if we were practicing female hairstyles. There's no reason why not."

"Yeah, a girl," she says, getting bored with her own joke.

"You're the one I want" —aiming a kiss at her lips and making do with an ear.

"Snip, snip," she says.

She lets him kiss her on the mouth.

After a minute she pulls away. "If you cheat on me with your other girlfriend, I'm going to yank her hair out!" She knocks the wig off. "See how ugly she is!"

Crow doesn't know how to deal with her when she's in this mood. She pretends she doesn't want it, but really she wants it, even more than he does. The wig is a dark pool on the tiled floor.

She pokes the torso, which is plump with paper, like a rat's nest.

"Did I ever tell you what happened on The Dragon Raises His Head day?" he says. "We had special long hours, so the parents could bring their kids in for their first haircut. Well, this guy came in. It was after dark and he was drunk. He asked to have his head shaved like a baby, with a peach-tuft at the front! I said no way, but Doggy and Chubby, they gave him what he asked for!"

"Yeah, you told me that story before, Crow. What happened to him? Is he still walking around with a peach-tuft?"

He looks at the clock. "Do you think another customer will turn up?"

She goes to the OPEN sign on the door, and turns it over to CLOSED.

"Crow," she says, "In my lunch hour I was on Chang'an Avenue, between the Ministry of Commerce and Tongren Hospital, and there was like a million of you roosting on the poplars. Crows—get it? Crows on the trees! Crows everywhere!"

He sings the chorus from a song that was a hit a few years back. *The crow solves the crow's problems, and I solve mine.* It used to be his number-one song; it's where his nickname comes from.

"A street cleaner was cleaning up the bird shit, and a crow shit right on top of his head!"

"Hey, we've all got to do it somewhere!"

It's frustrating. He lives in a dorm with the other apprentices, and she lives with her parents. If they were caught having sex after hours in the barbershop, he'd be fired. Sometimes they go to an abandoned truck that an apprentice, Dandruff, told him about, which is parked behind a warehouse by the Fifth Ring Road. There's cardboard taped over the windows, so nobody can see in. But he has to pay Dandruff every time he uses it, and it smells of all the people who've been there before. In summer there's a place screened by a linden tree in the park; it won't be long till it's warm enough. But you never know who might poke their nose in—a homeless person, or a druggie, or even a cop. It's weird: the danger turns Big Eyes on, and that turns him on. Someday, after his apprenticeship is over, he'll have a salon of his own. There'll be marble and chandeliers, and a bookcase with real books, and wealthy businessmen will bring their mistresses in for the latest styles from the fashion magazines, and he'll have a dozen apprentices to do his bidding.

He sits at the desk and goes through the takings—cash and credit receipts. Master Cao trusts him to do this. He taps figures into a calculator.

While he's doing the accounts, she fits a pair of plastic ear-covers on him. These are for people who are having their hair dyed, so their ears don't get dyed too. She stands back to admire her creation. "You're an alien from another planet,

Crow." She makes an eerie science-fiction noise. Then she flicks the ear-covers off, and they lie on the ground.

"What happens to all the cut-off hair?" she says. "There must be tons and tons. Do they make wigs out of it? Do they make one huge, giant wig?"

"They turn it into fertilizer. That's what Master Cao said. But Doggy said there was a story online about how it's turned into soy sauce."

"I wouldn't eat soy sauce made from human hair. Would you, Crow?"

"There's something wrong," he says.

"It's disgusting," she says.

"Fifty yuan short!"

"That can't be right. Count again."

He takes an abacus from a drawer, and double-checks. "Fifty fucking yuan! It was that out-of-towner, that's who it was! He had an accent like he was from Taiwan, and we all know what they're like! I gave him change of a hundred-yuan bill, but I bet it was only a fifty!"

"Are you sure?"

"Master Cao will take it out of my wages!"

"You poor thing." She repeats this with a Taiwanese accent, *"You poor thing."* She perches on his knee and strokes his hair.

"The Taiwanese stole my fifty yuan and he spent it on a hooker!"

"The other day a woman came into the boutique, and she chose a Scarlett O'Hara dress with puffy sleeves, and she tried to pay with a bunch of hundred yuan bills. But Mrs. Huang scratched Mao's head. On the real bill the hair's got texture, but on the fakes it's totally flat." Big Eyes mimics furious Mrs. Huang; she spits on the floor. "'Pei! I'm not taking your toilet paper.'" She gazes in a mirror, admiring her dramatization. She digs her fingers into her boyfriend's scalp. "Mrs. Huang pinned the fake bill on the wall, as a warning." She thinks about it. "It's like when farmers shoot a crow, they hang it up to warn off other crows."

Crow pushes her off his lap. He triple-checks the receipts, using paper and pen this time. Still the figures don't add up. He stands. His layered hair is fluffed up like a frightened bird's plumage. He swings his right arm back— "Don't do it!" she shrieks, "Stop, Crow!"—as, with a mighty groan, open-palmed, the way some people slap tree trunks to strengthen their qi, he launches into the side of a steel shelving unit.

The mirror vibrates. The reflection of the apprentice barber and the boutique assistant shivers. Foreseeing what will happen, she covers her eyes with her hands, peeking through. Everything seems to be developing in slow motion, like an earthquake on TV. A shelf tilts. A comb slides till it meets a brush, and the two journey together. Then the entire shelving unit buckles. Cans of hairspray and bottles of shampoo, scissors and razors, comb after brush after comb, the special foil they use for highlights, different kinds of gel, talcum powder, scalp cream, a hairdryer, a can of pineapple beer, several glossy magazines, and Da Shan, and the actual shelves come tumbling down.

Crow jumps back. Items smash against his face and neck and chest. A metal shelf lands on his foot.

She wills herself to be far from here—a mountain pass, the snow deep, and the sky an eternal blue.

He hops, gasping, clutching his ankle. He loses his balance and, half-collapsing half on purpose, bumps to the ground, and he ends up not exactly cross-legged, ringed by fallen objects like a child surrounded by his toys.

"Are you all right, Crow?"

"Of course I'm not fucking all right!"

"You've got blood on your face," she says calmly. During minor crises Big Eyes acts girlish and incompetent. More than once, when her feet ached after walking in high heels, she sat down on the sidewalk and refused to go one step further, which infuriated her boyfriend, but she's sure it excited him too.

"Never mind my face. My foot!"

She crouches and undoes his left shoe. Down with his sock. "Your ankle's swollen, Crow."

"I've broken something."

"Not broken, no."

"Maybe I need to go to the hospital? How am I going to pay? Master Cao will fire me!"

"It's not your fault."

"There are a hundred people out there, competing to be an apprentice barber."

"What does it matter? You don't cut hair with your ankle!"

"I'm on my feet all day long."

"You could use a stool."

"No customer wants their hair done by a man with a limp."

She helps him up, supporting his weight on her arms, and like a customer he sits in a chair. She takes a paper towel and wipes blood and shampoo off his face.

"There, there, Crow." She pouts. "You look so manly."

He shuts his eyes and inhales, in pain as if as in pleasure.

"We're going to have to put everything back on the shelves," she says.

"*You're* going to put everything back, Big Eyes. I can hardly. . . . This is the worst day of my life!"

It seems Big Eyes and Crow are already married in Heaven, for the same thought enters their heads simultaneously. Impossible to say which of the two first came up with the scheme.

"I feel like somebody mugged me, Big Eyes," he says, while she says, "You look like somebody mugged you, Crow."

"Thieves . . ." he says.

". . . broke in . . ." she says.

". . . just as I was counting the takings . . ."

". . . and they were all over you . . ."

". . . before I could stop them. They stole the fifty yuan from the cash register."

"They stole *everything* from the register," she corrects him. She takes the entire stash of money and puts it in her handbag. "You fought back. You were a hero!"

He cocks his head to one side, like a hero in a kung fu movie, and performs a martial arts gesture. "The evil-doers will not escape my vengeance!"

"Sheeeh," she says, the way heroes do, to emphasize the forcefulness of their attack.

"Master Cao can't fire me, not after I defended his barbershop. He'll have to cover my medical bills, too."

"He should give you a reward, Crow!" She giggles. "He should give you a medal!"

He rubs his chin. "We're going to have to decide what the thieves looked like."

"Yes, and how many of them there were."

"Three." He counts them off on his fingers. "Number One had his hair gelled in spikes. Number Two was a big man with a goatee. And the third . . . natural waves."

"Wavy hair? You mean, Number Three was from . . . somewhere like Xinjiang?"

"He was a white man."

She thinks about this. "Yes, I can see that."

"You were there, Big Eyes. You can back me up."

She pats a tissue on a cheek wound. "They say that losing a little blood is good for your health."

"You're going to back me up, Big Eyes, with Master Cao and everyone."

"Your blood type is AB, isn't it, Crow?"

"And you're O, the Universal Donor. Our bloods are compatible."

She picks up Da Shan. She kisses it on the "mouth," and bites it, and spits out a chunk. She puts the Styrofoam in place on the dummy and drops the wig on top.

"I turned up at the end, just as the baddies were running away," she concludes. "I mean, I saw them in the distance, but I wasn't . . . a fantastic hero like you, Crow, you did it all on your own! *Adorable!*"

*

An hour later, Crow and Big Eyes are at the police station. They're giving their version to a pair of detectives. They're aware of themselves as actors, improvising their life story—as even wholly sincere truth tellers do, under interrogation.

Detective Wang, a rumpled, middle-aged man, is in charge. His deputy, Detective Zhao, is taking notes.

The detectives concentrate on Crow, the injured one, the seeming victim. "Tell us exactly what happened," Wang says in a bored voice. "Begin at the beginning, and go on from there."

Crow describes how he was alone in the barbershop, tidying the place, sweeping up the hair—and suddenly the door swung open, and there in front of his very eyes. . . . As he makes up the story, he feels his girlfriend communicating with him telepathically, encouraging him, elaborating his account, taking it in ways beyond what he would have thought of. He describes the normality of it and the horror. How he was doing his job, the sequence of tasks, things he's done hundreds of times before. . . . The electric fan was blowing down his neck, and it swiveled away, and it blew at him again. . . . He had this weird intuition of doom . . . it was like in a computer game when you enter the mysterious cavern . . . it was like the iron band around the head of the Monkey King getting tighter and tighter. . . . And suddenly, yes, suddenly. . . . It's as much as he can do not to break down and cry, as in his telling of it the three terrible gangsters charge into the shop, slamming and stamping, screaming at him. He can see them in his mind's eye— Spiky and Goatee and White Guy too. He tried to fight them off singlehandedly, one ordinary barber against three mortal enemies, sidestepping, kicking. . . . To illustrate this, his voice wobbles and his hands twitch in fly-swatting gestures—a miniaturized reenactment of the epic battle. The three enemies grow as he speaks, like shadows projected on a wall—vicious Spiky, sneering Goatee, and White Guy shouting *fuck off*. . . . And then, just then, when he was on the point of passing out, when he literally might have died, along came his girlfriend . . .

The older detective says almost nothing, grunting occasionally on a descending note. The younger detective types into a computer.

It's true, Crow thinks, he really might have died. That's the most important part of his story, he wasn't lying about that at all. His left ankle is no longer hurting, and now that he is aware of this absence, it does hurt after all.

Meanwhile Big Eyes is assessing her chances. She hid the banknotes inside Da Shan's torso. One thousand, three hundred eighty-two yuan. Master Cao would never look there. But one of the other apprentices might find it. They're not stupid, Dandruff and Doggy. Even Chubby is not as stupid as all that.

When the narration is over, Detective Wang asks Crow if he could pick the thieves out, if he saw them again.

Crow didn't expect this question. It's a trick. If he says no, it'll seem he's not sure of his testimony. But if he says yes, he might be put to the test. They'll have him stand behind a one-way mirror, and on the other side the suspects will be lined up. There'll be an innocent man with gelled spikes, and another innocent man with a goatee, and maybe even a white man—and Crow will have to say, *Yes, he did it! He's the one! And him too!* "Probably," he says. "Maybe not."

"And what about the guy with the wavy hair," Detective

Zhao pipes up. "Are you sure he was a foreigner? We don't get many foreign crooks around here."

"I . . . I think so."

"Maybe he had the eyelid operation to look like a white man? Or maybe he was from Xinjiang?"

"That's what *I* said," says Big Eyes.

Zhao says, "Ah, so you did see him?"

"I saw him," she says. "It was just like Crow . . . just like my friend said."

"Up close? Close enough to see his eyelids? Close enough to tell he was from Xinjiang? Before you said you only saw the crooks from a distance?"

Before Big Eyes can find an answer, Wang holds up a hand like a traffic cop. "Enough, now." He hustles Crow into a small windowless room. Big Eyes is taken to the reception area and told to stay there until further notice.

The two detectives hunch in Number 2 Common Room. There's a counter with a microwave flanked by an orange and a bottle of baijiu, as if a shrine. The ghost of a mosquito coil shrivels on a blue-and-white dish. On the wall half of a patriotic slogan (WITHOUT THE COMMUNIST PARTY . . .) is visible; the rest is obscured by a taped-up printout of the license numbers of stolen vehicles. The detectives drink tea.

"What do you think?" Wang says.

"Sexy," Zhao says.

"They're all like that, these days," Wang says. "Every girl, everywhere. Lipstick, mascara . . . skirt up to here . . ."

"She's too good for him."

"All women are too good for all men. That's what my wife says."

"Ha. That's what my wife says too."

"My daughter's going to be sixteen in May. And do you know what she posted as her profile picture?"

"What?"

"You're never going to guess."

"I can guess."

"She altered the pic so half of her is in bed, and the rest of her is on the ceiling!"

"No. Really? Which half is where?"

"And in another pic, she's got an arm missing! It's not just her, it's all her friends. It's the fashion to look mutilated. Heaven didn't make them cripples—why do they do it to themselves?"

"We didn't do that when I was young."

"We didn't have the internet, when I was young."

There's a pause while the two of them contemplate that bygone era.

Eventually the younger detective says, "The barber?"

"Guilty as hell."

"Yes, guilty."

"Who does he think he is—Jackie Chan?"

"He thinks he's Jackie Chan!"

"My daughter's best friend, on her profile pic she's in slices. The caption is 'Death by a Thousand Cuts.'"

"More tea?" says Zhao, pouring from the pot into his superior's cup.

They touch the rims of their cups.

"Good stuff," says Zhao.

"Of course it's good stuff. Pu'er. It's a gift from a businessman from Yunnan. I did him a favor."

The detectives drink the aromatic tea, and stare dreamily.

Wang leans forward. "Let me tell you what really happened. A guy. A cute girl. And what's the third element? . . . It's a love triangle, obviously! She's been cheating on him with one of the other barbers! It's been going on for months, but her boyfriend only just found out. So what does he do? He challenges his rival to a duel—a scrappy fist fight, whatever. The two barbers, they fight over her. They wrestle, they tussle, they punch and kick, they fight so hard they wreck the shop. Young love!"

"We throw the book at him?"

"Ah, just enough to scare him. Teach him a lesson. We'll nail him on some minor charge."

"Like what?"

"Wasting police time."

"And her?"

"She's not important." Wang thinks: *I can't take care of everybody.*

"No charge for the girl at all?"

"Let her go and break a few more hearts."

Zhao heats up extra water in the microwave; it's quicker than using the kettle. If the barber lets me have a go with his girlfriend, he fantasizes, I could do him a favor. He watches the glass of water rotate slowly in the buzzing machine. Meanwhile Wang worries about his daughter. The school complained: she was caught selling copies of exam answers to other students. Why did she do that? She's not some illegal migrant lurking by the rail tracks! She doesn't need the money. He gives her everything she asks for.

"Hmm. What's our game plan, now?" Zhao calls over, as he gingerly extracts the hot glass, gripping it in a paper towel. "We interrogate the suspects separately? See if they corroborate each other's story?"

"No point. We *know* they're liars."

"Liars, yes."

"My wife reads mystery novels. She tells me about them in bed. There's always a crime at the beginning, and the detective spends the whole novel looking for clues, and on the last page he finds the solution. But in real life, you often don't even know whether a crime's been committed, and you've got a million other cases on your list. You've got to deal with stuff when it's in front of you, or else it all piles up. It's like washing dishes."

Zhao pours the boiling water on the damp leaves, refreshing them. "Washing dishes," he echoes.

"The barber will confess."

"He's got to confess."

"The only question is," Wang says, not looking up, "who'll squeeze the confession out of him? Me or you?"

Zhao stutters.

Wang produces a one-yuan coin. "Which side? Number or flower?"

Zhao responds.

Wang flips the coin. It lands near the edge of the desk, wobbles, rolls off, ends up on the floor. They peer down. The chrysanthemum side is up.

"You win," Wang says. "It's your turn to interrogate the perp."

Zhao feels he's being railroaded, made to do the dirty work. If the number side had been on top, Wang would have told him he'd lost, and that would have been given as the reason he had to do the interrogation. Ah, he's in no position to argue with his superior. He says, "What about the money?"

"Money?" Wang says in a distorted voice like a crosstalk comedian, as if money were an exotic and humorous concept.

"The money that went missing from the barbershop. The money they claim the thieves stole."

"Ha!"

"Do we nail the sucker on a theft charge, too?"

"Forget about the money." The older man sighs. "Money comes and money goes. Once you start worrying about money, there's no end to it."

*

In their separate zones within the police station, Big Eyes and Detective Wang sit alone. Each is trying to listen (though the interrogation room is soundproofed) or at least to sense what is going on.

Big Eyes thinks she hears voices. The voices are coming from different directions: up through the floorboards and down from the ventilation shaft, as well as flowing from the walls. One of the voices is her boyfriend's, the other the younger detective's (he was quite good looking, she reckons). She can't make out any specific words.

Wang likewise imagines he hears the interrogation: not what is being said but the familiar rhythm of it.

She concentrates, staring at her own hand—the pretty fingernails, the good-luck qilin tattoo on her wrist—but she can't help thinking about the stash. All those denominations in subtle, hard-to-copy shades, like a display of sophisticated lingerie. If only she were wealthy and beautiful, like those models in the magazines! They live the glamorous life! Last winter there was a photospread showing a stunning model in a panda suit riding an electric bicycle around Beijing. The fad took off: now anywhere you go, you might see a panda on a bike.

She'll return to the barbershop. She'll find a time when her boyfriend's not there (likely as not he'll be in jail—no problem, then). She'll flirt if she has to, tell some barber his coiffure is *adorable*. . . . And when nobody's around, she'll take off the Styrofoam head, and she'll plunge her hand deep inside the sweatshirt (she can almost feel the texture of it: the taut cloth with its papery stuffing) and she'll draw out the secret treasure. All the lovely cash clutched in her fist. She won't need to count: it'll all be there.

One thousand three hundred eighty-two yuan.

Enough for a one-way ticket to anywhere in China.

She's a Beijinger. And it's true what they say: the world comes to Beijing. But you can't live your whole life in the place you were born.

Where, then?

Tibet, she thinks. She saw a documentary on TV. The mountains, the monasteries, the yaks . . . how the indigenous people are welcoming the economic development brought by the Chinese government. Maybe it's not all true, but half true or a quarter true is true enough. Tens of thousands of Han Chinese men are migrating there, to the new frontier, some of them getting lucky and striking it rich. Plenty of men and not enough women. That's the place for her. She knows what she's worth. She's pretty, but not especially pretty by Beijing standards. In Tibet she'll be a beauty. She's smart but not too smart. That's what most frontier men are looking for. Maybe she'll settle down there; maybe she'll move on; maybe decades in the future she'll come back to the capital, a rich widow with a handsome son. The documentary said that traditionally one Tibetan woman would marry several husbands. Well, who knows?

Wang heaves his chair over. He covers his eyes with his forearm. His left ear is squashed against the wall. This afternoon he got a call from a precinct in Dongcheng District. His daughter was caught trying to pass fake money at a clothing store. He arranged for her to be released without charge, of course. But there's a limit to his powers. If she keeps getting into trouble, he won't be able to save her. She'll shame herself and shame the entire family. He doesn't understand the world these days—so many negative influences out there: gangs and cults, foreign trends, wicked sites on the internet, scurrilous news sheets slandering the most important people in China. . . . Not like when he was her age; there were bad elements, too, but at least you knew where you stood. Nowadays—who's a praiseworthy innovator and who's a counter-revolutionary? Who's a shrewd entrepreneur and who's a thief? A daughter should obey her father. But if she doesn't, what can he do? What can any man do?

Eventually both Big Eyes and Wang think they hear it.

Hear something, anyway. *A thud, and a squeal . . . A thud and a squeal . . .* A junior detective forcing some kind of truth out of an apprentice barber? A confession of sorts, a story we can agree on? . . . Or are they listening to the heart pumping blood around their own body, the breath in and out of their own lungs?

THE HUMAN PHONOGRAPH

And as a figure in a reflective helmet and articulated suit half-walks half-floats over the unreal surface she make-believes he is her husband, and the moon itself could perfectly well be Qinghai province for all anybody can tell, and one of the other translators, one who specializes in English, says Mr. Armstrong is saying, "A small step for man, a large step for man" and she shades her eyes with her hands so nobody can see her cry.

It has been seven years.

There are thoughts that cannot be spoken but can only be sung.

The summons comes in the form of a telegram to the secretary of her work unit. She has a week in which to pack.

They met in 1961 when she was a senior majoring in Russian at the Foreign Studies University and he was finishing his PhD in geology. They married and less than a year later he received the order. He was being sent to the far northwest to investigate a certain terrain—as much as he could say. He would remain there indefinitely. She was forbidden to accompany him. As if he were being sent into exile, or they both were, but it was presented as a reward, an opportunity to Serve the People. . . . And in October 1964, Year of the Dragon, Mao proclaimed that China has the Bomb.

There is a photograph (it will not be made public till years later, after his death, and by then she will be back in Beijing) of scientists in identical suits raising their clenched left fists in a loyalty salute, on an open plain, under a bright sun. He is third from the left, overexposed. Posed, of course. In reality they would have been cowering in a shelter, plugs in their ears and goggles over their eyes, while the earth shuddered.

The Bomb is a defense against the Soviet Union, and the irony is they helped us make it in the first place. As a schoolgirl she was taught to honor our fraternal ally. The class sang "Katyusha" and "My Land." By the time she went to university, Russian was the language of the enemy. We understand them in order to defeat them.

Once a week she sends a letter to the base's deliberately bland address: Factory 221, Mining Area 210, Qinghai. He replies when he can. He is forbidden to describe his work; he is forbidden even to describe the rocks beneath his feet. He writes about the weather. *Today the temperature dropped to -20°. We are keeping warm in our goose down coats.* (He is thinking of putting his arms around her, warming her!) . . . *Today is a typical summer day, which is about the same temperature as spring in Beijing.* (Here in the city the heat is oppressive. . . . He is thinking of spring!)

Let the long gray boulevards of Beijing be memorials to themselves. Already the herds of cyclists, blurry on their Phoenixes and their Forevers, creak like ghosts. It is the final morning. In the courtyard of her collective housing the children are playing a game in which they hide, making themselves as silent and invisible as possible. She is permitted to take one suitcase.

July 28, 1969.

She sets out from Beijing railroad station, and it is a five-day journey to Lanzhou in Gansu province. From there she is transferred to a special military train that goes to Qinghai. Everyone else is male and in uniform. The windows of the cars are shuttered so the passing land cannot be seen. She might as well be blind. If only she'd brought a novel or poetry. . . but she didn't dare take any book apart from the Chairman's thoughts. By day she sweats; by night she huddles under her quilt. She listens. The engine's rhythmic clanking and energetic shushing. Sometimes for no apparent reason the train pauses for hours. The burble of a river. A dog's bark. A bleating and a human shout. . . And on the eighth morning she wakes and she is the only passenger in her car, and she hears and feels the shift as she is shunted onto a track leading to the secret base, and that afternoon at last her doors are opened and here she is.

Grassland, stretching forever. A shocking blue sky. Squat cement buildings that look as if they were put up yesterday and will crumble tomorrow. Soldiers in a chain unload crates from the train and transfer them to parked trucks, each man passing his burden to the next man along.

She is being observed by a thin, hatless man in canvas army shoes and a creased blue suit. His face is sunburnt. He says her full name, as if approaching a stranger. His voice is strained, yet he has an unexpected air of authority.

Not to be outdone in formality, she greets him—prefacing his name with the salutation "Comrade."

He scarcely resembles the photo of him that she carries everywhere, next to her work unit documents.

She has changed too. Who's to say that she isn't an impostor herself?

Seven years.

They get into an open-framed vehicle, and a sergeant drives them. Her husband behaves like a considerate stranger. Is she hot? Is she cold? No and no. Is she tired from the journey? She is. Would she like some water? Not really, but she replies she is thirsty, to be polite, and he raises a flask in a camouflage cover, and she sips, her lip touching where his lip has been. A sparrow hawk wheels high above them.

The vehicle brakes sharply; husband and wife are jolted against each other. This is the married quarters, he says. And before she can ask her question, he answers it, You are the only civilian wife.

He leads her in. A small room, which she could use as a

study, if she likes, and another room with little more than a bed in it. The sergeant deposits her suitcase, and leaves them.

They look slightly past each other.

He draws the improvised curtain—blackout cloth suspended from a string.

The dry air will crack your lips, he says. It is advisable to wear lipstick at all times.

Lipstick? Lipstick is bourgeois deviationism; it hasn't been obtainable in Beijing for years.

He points with his foot at a cardboard box containing steel tubes of lipstick that resemble bullets. Hundreds of tubes. Enough for a lifetime of red lips.

They sit on the bed, at opposite ends. They had nine months of married life until he was exiled; they addressed each other as old wifey and old hubby, playing at marriage.

She unscrews a tube and applies it, wriggling her lips and pouting to spread the redness evenly. It tastes like perfumed machine oil, and perhaps it is.

He undresses her.

His fingers consider her, inscribing target areas on her skin.

For the first year or so after he left, she dreamed of him every night, and she would wake to the astonishment of his absence. And then, gradually, like stars in an urban dawn, he faded out of her dreams.

She has no specific memory of making love to him; it wasn't something separate from their life: it *was* their life.

He has her lie down; her head is where feet would normally be. Eyes closed, she watches him through her nostrils. Qinghai stretches from the great saltwater lake in the south to the plateau on the Tibetan border. The geologist sets out on an exploratory trip. He examines her, investigates her, takes a core sample . . . and as Qinghai thrashes and screams, she is a tiny figure within the province of herself . . . she is cast back to Beijing, to her desk at the Institute, with its precious window looking out to the north—but this version of the city is ecstatic, distorted: instead of a flat street with cyclists, there is a broad highway lifted high in the air along with extra highways looping around, all rich with candy-colored cars, and instead of a vista of a horizontal apartment building, glittery towers stretch up into a misty heaven, and passersby dressed in bright wisps stare back, not seeing her. . . . Once again she is the terrain of Qinghai. . . . She yearns for impossible Beijing. . . . She is a wife on a hard bed, a husband's weight holding her where she is.

The following morning she reports to her job, the one he found for her. She is not here as a wife (there is no such category) but as essential technical support. She has a chair and a desk of her own, army issue, with the characters for "librarian" painted in red on the underside. The collection is excellent. The textbooks are mostly in Russian, from the 1950s. In the geology section she notices a much-thumbed

Classification and Identification of Metamorphic Rocks by the great Davidovitch himself, who taught her husband. Also there are journals and preprints; there are blueprints and technical specifications with Cyrillic markings; there is a file of secret photographs of Soviet installations. And she is astonished to find, on an open stack, an entire bookshelf loaded with classic literature: Tang Dynasty poems, in which the male author speaks in a female voice; the erotic novellas of Li Yu; Pu Songling's horror stories, composed in the decadence of the Ming Dynasty.... Foreign books too, in several languages: English, French, German ... and yes, her beloved Russian; here is Pushkin (once she was Tatiana, besotted with Yevgeniy) and Gogol and Dostoevsky.... How did these books find their way here? And how come they're still permitted? Anywhere else in China, anybody caught reading these would be denounced. So she learns that Factory 221 is not like anywhere else in China. Ringed with barbed wire and guarded by T-59 tanks, it is the securest of prisons and paradoxically it has the most freedom. The Cultural Revolution does not apply here. The scientists are privileged exceptions—more valuable than giant pandas. They are supplied with their special diet, whatever is needed to nourish their rare brains.

Men wander in and find excuses to chat with her. So you're the librarian, they say, you're just what we need. There are a handful of other women here, scientists in their own right. When they come into the library they avoid her or abbreviate their conversations. The library here is not hushed like those at the Institute or the university; men smile at her and reminisce about the heroic era in the early history of the base, when the scientists lived in army tents and survived on mutton and barley buns . . .

A fluid dynamicist, Jin, recalls the 1950s. Mao and Stalin shook hands, and behold the Friendship Hotel in Beijing (*Hotel Druzhba*) was filled with Soviet advisors. Jin was friends with Vanyushin, whom he jokingly nicknamed Wang Yuqin; they went on long walks together and talked about poetry. Then Mao quarreled with Stalin, and all the advisors had to leave. Jin is short with poor teeth; he shows her a photograph of himself and Vanyushin, a tall blond man, in the Temple of Heaven.

That evening there is a concert in the dining room. Under the portrait of Mao, a physicist plays Chopin. Followed by a string quartet—the violinists are mathematicians, the viola is an electrical engineer, and the cellist with his shock of white hair studied at Harvard in the 1930s and brought nuclear chemistry to China. Afterward, drinks are served. Not alcohol, of course, which is forbidden on the base, but an instant sour plum juice made from a powder dissolved in water.

The name of the first Bomb test was Operation Qilin. The qilin is a mythical creature with the body of a deer, the tail of an ox, the hooves of a horse, and a single horn. And indeed there is just such a creature, rather bedraggled, created by a taxidermist, just inside the main entrance to the dining room. To the scientists it is so familiar they pay it no special attention: there's a scarf on the horn and somebody's coat is draped over its haunch. According to legend, if you burn the horn like a torch (What is it really—an antelope's?), you will see the future. The qilin is said to manifest only in the reign of a benevolent emperor.

She is an object of fascination. Perhaps one day she, too, will become as unremarkable as this qilin.

How come her husband is not more fascinated? Or say that he is, but he doesn't show it. That night, in their bedroom, he brushes his teeth and makes love to her. Soon he goes to sleep, flat on his back, his arms at his side. There is a little red on his chin and nose—lipstick transferred from her lips. He does not snore. His eyelids do not flicker. He does not exclude her from the bed, but there is no natural way to arrange her body next to his either. A not very married man.

This goes on for weeks. Nothing is the matter, exactly. He mentions that he is not in the best of health, but he seems fit enough. Most of the scientists are a little overweight (the food is plentiful but not tasty), but he remains skinny, no matter how much he consumes.

He has secrets, of course. There are things he cannot even whisper in bed.

And then he tells her he's going on an expedition. He'll

be leaving at dawn and will be back before dusk. The privilege of geology. Nobody else is allowed to go off-base. He'll be exploring possible sites for . . . but already he's said too much.

She gets up early and sees him off. He's driving a Soviet motorcycle, a Ural M-72, a vintage model from the war. In the sidecar is his assistant, a short dark man, locally recruited, named Chodrak, or, in Chinese, Kuohui. The assistant carries a rock hammer. Her husband fastens his goggles, the engine roars, and away the men go.

She spends the day in the library stacks, arranging the books. There is rumored to be a cat that roams the base, a wild creature named by the physicists "Schrödinger." Pussy, pussy, pussy . . . she whispers.

He returns after midnight. What happened? she asks, and he offers some explanation that is not quite an explanation, how there was a delay in a mountain pass. . . . There's more work to be done; he'll have to go back soon. He has a blaze of pale dust on his forehead and seems both weaker and more excited, feverish. You should take care of yourself, she says, is there anything I can do for you? But all he wants now is her body. Despite his tiredness he must have her. She keeps her eyes open this time and sees the thin, sunburnt man caressing her, and she feels that somehow he is cheating on her even as he makes love to her, until finally she closes her eyes and sees again that impossible Beijing with its luminous billboards and hears a throbbing music unlike any that exists in real life, a rhythmic skeleton of a song bedecked with a jangle of rhymes.

Can I come with you on your next trip? she asks him the following morning.

No.

Why not?

You don't have permission. Besides, there's only room for one passenger in the sidecar.

But why can't I be your assistant, instead of Chodrak? You could train me. How difficult can it be?

You're needed at the library.

I'm needed with *you*.

She touches his narrow chest. His bony ribs.

He changes into everyday clothes.

I'll be going on an expedition again next week . . .

You mean, I can come with? I can come with or I cannot come with? What do I have to learn? Teach me, old hubby.

He scratches his chest. He says, Sing for me.

What?

Sing me a song. Any song.

A weird request. Music? From her? He knows perfectly well she has no voice. Well, if her husband wants her to sing, then sing she must. What, then? There are those songs she's heard over and over again, played through the loudspeakers at the Institute: "Rely on the Helmsman While Sailing the Sea" . . . "The Red Army Crosses a Thousand Mountains

and Ten Thousand Rivers, Yearning for a Moment of Rest."
. . . But surely he'd prefer something more personal. It's not
as if they ever had a song that was *their* song. Unlike other
courting couples, they never listened to jazz together, back
when it was permitted; they never went ballroom dancing.
She chooses something she was taught in Russian class, "The
Song of the Volga Boatmen." *Yo heave ho. Once more, once
more again, still once more. Yo heave ho . . .*

He lowers his gaze. He says with conviction, No, you do
not have the talent to be my assistant.

Over the following weeks he, accompanied by Chodrak,
goes on several expeditions. Sometimes he even stays away
overnight. Always he comes back weaker and yet refreshed;
always he insists on making love to her immediately. What
could she complain about? He is attentive, considerate, and
he obviously finds her physically attractive. Yet he is not quite
present, like a dissatisfied ghost.

In early September, for the first time there is frost on the
ground. The winter is about to begin: a poor season for a
geologist. That afternoon he leads her into his laboratory. It
is a sectioned-off portion of what had once been a hangar,
high with an angled ceiling, and with no natural light. The
storage bins are repurposed from ammunition containers.
An array of scoops and picks and chisels and pry-bars hang
upside-down like bats. She sits on a stool next to a polarizing
microscope, her head bowed as if imitating its posture. The

assistant is in the corner, squatting, removing rock samples from a bin and sorting them.

Her husband addresses her as if delivering an ethnographic lecture. He describes the varied peoples of Qinghai: those of Han Chinese, Mongolian, and (a glance at Chodrak) Tibetan descent, as well as indigenous tribes such as the Tu (whose language is related to Mongolian but whose customs are similar to Tibetans') and the Sala who are Muslim.

What's this to do with geology, she thinks.

The peoples interact, he says, they influence each other. In the course of my exploration, I encounter peasants. We exchange food and drink. They give me directions. They understand the earth on which they live.

He adds, Sometimes they sing.

What?

The men and the women, they sing to each other.

Folk song? Is this what you mean?

Yes.

Like the songs we were taught in school?

Not like the songs we were taught in school. It's called Hua'er. A man sings it to a woman, a woman sings it to a man. They keep it up all night long. He confesses, I cannot sing myself. I have no memory for music. But my assistant, I call him The Human Phonograph.

He raises a finger, like a conductor.

Chodrak—without getting up, without adjusting his

squat, without any change of expression—sings. His dark face is as opaque as ever. She cannot understand the words (whatever language this is, it's not Chinese), but the tune is remarkable, soaring and tumbling like the mountains of Qinghai. It does not last long. In silence he continues sorting rocks.

The conductor raises his finger again.

Once again The Human Phonograph produces the same song, identical in every regard to his first performance. There are some odd pauses, places where he seems slightly out of tune, and she realizes these too are identical to his original rendition. Rather as when the Party reconstructed a schoolhouse in Hunan province where Mao studied as a young man, they restored the original crack in the roof through which rain dripped, and included a stuffed rat on the floor— so we should know what he went through, what made him who he is.

Silence again. Now she speaks out.

I want to hear it.

The song repeats a third time, precisely as before, with all the peaks and valleys.

In the middle of a bar, she barks, Stop!

The song stops.

Continue!

The song resumes from where it left off and completes itself. Her husband says, It's a Sala song. Which he translates:

The red morningstar lily is blossoming; it blooms radiantly. The young woman is ravishing; she has gorgeous eyebrows.

He says, The way it works, the first half of a Hua'er song is a description. The second half is an explanation. He looks down at his feet. I made something of a study of these songs, while you were away in Beijing. My hobby, you see.

This is the nearest he's come to telling her he loves her, that he missed her. And he was taking a risk for her sake too. Hua'er is surely illegal—bourgeois sentiment. The peasants are so isolated they don't understand it's against the law. But her husband knows. That's why he can't record them in any way except via The Human Phonograph. And Chodrak, too, wouldn't he be at risk? Might he betray his master? But he is too simple, too ignorant, to be aware of any danger.

Her husband signals The Human Phonograph, and a different song is heard. This time it's in a Chinese dialect, which she can follow. *For so long the thick grass has grown on the cliff; I could not cut it as the sickle is dull. For so long I have been in love with my girl; I could not tell her as I am shy.*

That night in bed, in the dark, she draws him to her. They lie side by side, and he tells her about his early days at Factory 221. How tough it was at first, the primitive conditions. But we had comradeship, everyone was in it together! He talks about the other geologists on his team, men like Four Eyes, and Badger, and Quartz, and Uncle Xu . . .

The names mean nothing to her; they're not here now. She asks what happened to them.

Ah, they're gone.

She hears the tension in his voice.

What is he implying? That they were dismissed? Were they denounced and punished in some way? Were they accused of being counter-revolutionaries?

He clarifies, They got sick.

And . . . ?

They're dead.

She realizes that the reason for his promotion, the reason he has the power to bring her here, is not because he is especially brilliant, but because he is the senior surviving geologist.

How come? she says, guessing the horrible answer even as she asks the question.

The usual thing.

What usual thing?

We observed Operation Qilin. We were too close. There was dust everywhere.

And you?

I'm lucky. The doctors say I could live for years.

Everyone waited for the lunar landing, in the lecture hall of the Institute. The English translator elucidated Mr. Armstrong's name; with his finger in the air he sketched the characters for *arm* and *strong*. And what about Mr. Aldrin, somebody asked, is his name auspicious too? But his name, like most names, signifies nothing, neither good nor bad.

She hears his slow breathing. He's fallen asleep. It wouldn't be right to wake him, and she can't sleep herself. She drifts along the edge, not quite dreaming . . . a snow-capped mountain . . . a mushroom cloud . . . a creature with the body of a man up to the neck and in place of a head the horn of an old-fashioned phonograph . . .

She wakes in the night. A sense of doom; and she recalls what her husband told her. What was she dreaming of? Not of him, so in that sense she was unfaithful.

Her dream is adapted from a story in *Collected Works of Anton Chekhov, Volume II,* which she's been reading in the library. It is about a bashful officer in the Tsarist army who is invited to a social gathering in a villa. He wanders into a dark room. A woman, supposing he's someone else, kisses him. . . . They never meet again.

In her dream version, she is the woman from that story. She is having an illicit affair. By mistake she kisses the shy, whiskery fellow. . . . She is shocked; then repulsed; then, struck by her own power, she goes in search of the original man she intended to kiss.

What a sadist the author is! It's just a story; the author can give it any ending he wants. Let the hero meet a suitable woman and they fall in love and they live happily ever after. But once it's published, the ending can no longer be changed.

When Chekhov wrote *The Kiss,* he was dying of tuberculosis. She understands him but does not forgive him.

He takes a turn for the worse. That September is the last time they make love, the last time he goes out on a geological expedition. He suffers during the long harsh winter; an oxygen cylinder hisses behind their bed. He is transferred to the base hospital.

She visits, and lies to him, as a wife should. She says, The doctors inform me you are getting better.

She thinks of Emperor Qin Shihuang, who was so determined to live forever that he took an elixir of immortality that contained mercury, and so brought about his own death—according to the account in *Records of the Grand Historian.*

As she does her work now there is a hush about her, appropriate for a librarian. Her calligraphy, *The earth is mutable; the sea becomes a mulberry orchard* (from Mao's "The People's Army Captures Nanjing"), has pride of place in the exhibition in the dining room.

He feels better, and then not better. In the spring he loses the ability to speak. He cannot communicate in any way.

Is he capable of seeing me? she asks a doctor.

No.

Can he hear me?

Possibly.

June 18, 1970. Her husband is in a private room. There is

another bed, not made up. She lies down on it, parallel to her husband.

His oxygen cylinder hiccups.

She was a girl gripping her grandmother's hand when the ancient wall around Beijing was demolished. She gazed through the refractions of dust at the naked, vulnerable city; swarms of volunteers took the rubble away.

I have brought you a gift, she says.

Chodrak is standing between them, facing neither. Impassive as ever, The Human Phonograph sings.

Come to the orchard if you would like to taste the cherries; there are thousands of summer flowers blooming. Do not be sad because we are parting; in a few days we will meet.

She sees the figure in the middle—Kuohui, whatever he goes by. From this angle, he could be almost any man in a peaked cap, a dark blue jacket. His eyebrows meet in the middle. She reaches out. Between finger and thumb she rubs the cheap "patriotic wool" of his jacket. She lifts a pocket flap; the concealed button is off-white.

She thinks of her husband, as he was on their wedding night.

She does not withdraw her touch.

Come to the orchard . . . he sings again.

She feels the warmth of the man, close by her face.

She shuts her eyes and enters her fabulous Beijing: she does not see a panorama of the steel-and-glass metropolis now, but rather a vast deep pit with many yellow-hatted workers swarming in and about it—where the foundations are to be established for the tallest of towers, that shall one day be built. And, playing in the background like film music, there is Hua'er. She hears another song . . . a third song . . . a fourth . . . in what might be Tibetan or Mongolian, Sala, or Tu . . . any of the numerous languages she does not know.

Colonel Li is sympathetic but unrelenting. It is impossible for her to stay at Factory 221.

She understands. She expected nothing else. There is no place for a single female non-scientist here.

She thinks of the legendary Peach Blossom Spring—the paradise that a fisherman once found by chance; he continued on his journey, and could never find it again.

She is given a week to pack.

On August 21, 1970, she is sent away. She is the passenger in a Fenghuang automobile, and she leaves along with other government vehicles. The convoy follows an indirect route across Qinghai, stopping at several military bases around Xining and a mining camp near Golmud. Through the rolled-up windows she sees the great saltwater lake, so vast it appears to be an ocean. She sees a mountain range to the north. . . . She identifies geological features (her husband taught her this skill): pillow lava and basalt; also greenish serpentinites and spilites: the ophiolites that prove this plateau was once an ocean floor, lifted up by subduction. Resting her hand on her belly she senses the motion within. She sees a flock of mountain sheep. She sees antelope who flee from the noise of the vehicles. She sees a distant shambling figure that might be a bear or a human. She sees a woman milking a yak, and wiping a little milk on her face, to whiten it. And at one point, along the pass that leads through to Gansu from where she will catch her train to Beijing, she sees a gathering of young people in traditional clothing; the women are carrying black umbrellas against the sun. The men and women pair off. She cannot hear through her window, but she supposes that each man is singing to his woman, and each woman to her man.

RECORDS OF THE GRAND HISTORIAN

It waves its paw, it waves and it waves—it's like that bouncing ball on the karaoke screen: whatever word the ball bounces on, that's what we've got to sing—and sometimes I've had all the waving I can take, and I just want to crack open the cat's bottom and yank the battery out, but I must never do that, because . . . because the cat's a lucky cat. Because the cat's a gift from a high-ranking cadre. The cadre owes me, I owe him. I give him a kickback, he gives me a cat; we're fair and square. Not that I believe in golden cats, but they say the golden cat brings luck even to people who don't believe in it.

I looked 'it up online, and guess what? The idea of the cat was imported from Japan, and we don't want the Japs pushing their superstitions down our throat, but on the other hand their luck is better than our luck, so why the hell not?

I wonder how many golden cats were blown up at Hiroshima.

It's the biggest project I've ever done. Will it succeed? Will it fail? Who knows? It's in a prime location in the Dongcheng District. Right now it's up to seventeen floors, just short of half its final height, and every day it goes up and up, and I go down and down into debt. People don't realize all the expenses involved. Even before you begin, there are the sweeteners to officials and to persons of power, you've got to wangle the necessary permits, and public security's got to be on your side, you don't get nothing for nothing. Then there's the land itself; you've got to deal with the previous owners, one way or another, buy them off, or pay the politicians to deal with it. And the price of cement is up, and don't talk to me about steel, and as for the workforce—the era when you could get migrants to slave for next to nothing is long past, believe you me. I have to import them personally from Sichuan, and I practically treat them like my own children, it's like I'm working for them. Would you like meat three times a day? It's a pleasure, gentlemen. Do you want me to serve you your traditional pickles? Whatever you'd like, gentlemen. Do you want me to equip you with work clothes and hard hats and goggles and respirators and turn a blind eye when you sell them on the black market? I'll go along with that, gentlemen. Do you want to work short hours and laze around on the job? Well, no, there I draw the line. You work your asses off, or else. I've got to bare my claws, or they'll think I'm Hello Kitty. I was a laborer once myself, I got my hands dirty. I don't mean I started right from the bottom—I grew up with some money and connections, sure—but I'm not one of those children of party chiefs who spend their entire lives in their air-conditioned Lamborghinis and have no idea what it's like in the real world.

My first job in the business, my mother's cousin hired me as a trainee bookkeeper. This is funny. I consistently failed math in high school. But Dad was a scientist, so Uncle Chan thought I had it in my genes. Then Uncle Chan realized that maybe I can't add up, but I'm good at bullshitting. I can persuade people that a shopping mall or a housing complex will appear on an empty lot. I can make it sound so real they're practically convinced it exists already, and they'll buy a share in it, sight unseen. Sometimes I can even convince myself.

I need to make a decision. I need a coin to toss.

This was how I got married, in fact. Lan was super keen on me, and it wasn't for my looks (I'm not saying I'm ugly, but I'm handsome in a short dark fat guy with eyebrows that meet in the middle kind of way) and she was loyal and tough and the most beautiful woman in China, and her mother got on with my mother (not many people get on with my mother). Flower-side of the coin, marry her; number-side, don't. *Go for it,* the coin said. I got down on my knees, "Will you be my beloved forever and ever?"

So what would you do in my position? I pass for wealthy, but if I liquidated everything today, I'd be four hundred million yuan in the hole. These are my options. One: Declare bankruptcy. I've got enough squirreled away, I'd still have a quality lifestyle. Two: Up the stakes. Borrow more, to keep the ball bouncing. An American connection of mine, George, put me in touch with Russian investors who are looking to launder their money; they buy a share in my business now, and I buy back their share at a discount at the end of the agreed period. A win-win for everybody. The problem is, the Chinese government doesn't permit foreigners to own a stake in my business, so George helped me set up a Variable Interest Entity, which is made up of three separate companies. There's a real estate company, which owns the physical property. Then there's a financial consultancy, which takes all the profits from the first company. These are both Chinese companies, in my name. And the third company, incorporated in Delaware, takes all the profits from the financial consultancy. The Russians get a share in the Delaware company. The fiction is: under Chinese law, the property belongs solely to me, whereas under American law some of it belongs to them. But the Russians are no pushovers. If I refused, or was unable, to pay them what they're owed, they wouldn't be able to sue me in China, so instead they'd have to shoot me. But what's the chance of my not paying them back on time?

Sometimes I cruise around Beijing in my BMW, and the city is made of ice cream and it's going to melt . . . . But my project, why shouldn't it be a winner? The name I'm giving it is Emperor Qin Tower. There used to be a row of apartment buildings here, put up in the 1960s, and beneath that a shelter for use in nuclear war. When I bought the property the shelter was inhabited by hundreds of illegal migrants. They had to move on. I did them a favor, spurring them to find a better future. Demolition comes next. A grand explosion. Dust and rubble. Then I excavate deep down, to lay my foundations.

The site looks vaguely military, the way they do. You go through the outer perimeter and the security gate, and you see a pool of mud plus a couple of big army tents that serve as a dining hall and as a storage area. The workers wear surplus infantry uniforms because they're cheap. (The PLA switched to uniforms with digitized patterns, so you can buy job lots of the old camo, supposed to blend in with a jungle in Vietnam or wherever.) I don't mean the workers dress like soldiers— they mix and match—maybe ragged fatigues combined with Warrior brand sneakers and a T-shirt advertising Kirin beer and plaid sleeve-protectors. It could be the HQ of a guerilla army in postapocalyptic Beijing. And there's a trailer dumped next to the dining tent, and me inside it with my reading glasses on, staring into the screen. On top of the monitor a golden cat waves its lucky paw. I'm not an accountant; I'm a builder at heart. I don't want to deal with spreadsheets. I'd rather be out there with a shovel in my hands, pitching in with my workers, belting out a shanty above the roar of the cement mixer, *Hi yo! Hi yo! Nobody told you to be poor!*

I hire a site manager, and I do his job on top of mine! You can't keep me away from the place.

I remember the old days when scaffolding was made of bamboo. Nowadays we use prefabricated components whenever we can. I went on a business trip to Taiwan, and they had robots that did the welding. I swear, the day will come when robots will do everything. We'll let the robots get on with it, and we'll come back in a year and there'll be a whole new city.

Number or flower?

Scrap the whole shebang, or pile up the debt?

The Russians, they gave me till midnight tonight, to make a decision.

You can't win every time. Lan's mother passed away after years of dialysis; the transplant operation was her last chance. The donated kidney didn't literally come from my own body, but I footed the bill, so in a way it did. I paid for the funeral too—no expense spared. A Buddhist monk did his thing, and my mother brought along a Christian priest, who passed around the bread and wine; might as well hedge your bets. Just as the chalice reached me, a journalist-for-hire, Kong, a connection of Lan's, stuck his camera in my face. He was supposed to be writing a story: PROMINENT REAL ESTATE DEVELOPER MOURNS AT MOTHER-IN-LAW'S FUNERAL; instead it looked more like REAL ESTATE SHYSTER GETS DRUNK AT MOTHER-IN-LAW'S FUNERAL. I said something to Lan I shouldn't have: "Would you have married me if I wasn't rich?" "Would you have married me if I wasn't beautiful?" And the funny thing is, in her sadness her beauty was hidden and I loved her all the more. She said, "I'd still love you if you weren't rich, but would you still love yourself if you weren't rich?" That night our son was conceived.

I take a puff of a cigarette. It's a fake that tastes just like a real Zhongnanhai, a gift from one of my associates. You know what they say: If you buy one fake cigarette, you're a fool. If you buy ten, you're smart. If you buy a hundred, you're rich. If you buy a thousand, you're in jail.

I leave the BMW in the parking garage. (It's the four-cylinder turbo version, built for speed. Call me crazy, but I don't have a driver.) I walk along. No coin on me. "Got change?" I ask a passerby, a hundred-yuan bill held out between finger and thumb. I try the next person, and the next. Everybody ignores me. They think I'm a beggar!

Here's a financial services office with a stretch of black marble in front, and a skateboarder is grinding along the edge, and behind him an old man is mopping the marble except now that I look again the man isn't mopping the marble, he's calligraphing characters on it with water. He grips his stick as if needing it to keep him upright. His cap is on the ground. I drop my hundred-yuan in, and I take out a one-yuan coin, and he's writing ONE SMALL STEP FOR INDIVIDUAL, ONE BIG STEP FOR NATION, and he doesn't even notice my generosity! Nobody notices! . . . And the skateboarder crashes to the sidewalk, and picks himself up, and tries all over again.

Into the site. I put on a hard hat. I take the elevator to the current highest level of Emperor Qin Tower. As I ascend my eyes are shut and I'm on a quest to the farthest reaches of China.

Seventeen floors up. Traffic throbs below like an orchestra tuning up. You can sort of see Tiananmen except for the smog. A red-billed blue-tailed magpie glides on a thermal.

I want to be on top.

I grab hold of the scaffolding, leading to the uncompleted eighteenth floor, and I monkey up it. (I hired a Taoist martial arts champion as a personal trainer; he's got me focusing on my qi.) The trick is to kid yourself you're on the ground; you're only going one story up, so how far can you fall?

I'm taller than anybody else!

Fumble for my coin.

Flick it . . .

Intending to catch it, but . . .

The smell of burning fills my nostrils, and while the coin falls down I fall upward . . . and for an instant Beijing shows itself as it might be—the stumps of gray buildings, roasted cars, human dust on the glassy earth . . .

Who knows where the coin lands? Who knows which side is up?

Yes, I should do the Russian deal!

No, I should not!

I balance on the edge . . .

I'll come back and flip another coin—good money after bad. My Taoist master would approve. Like when you lose an arrow, they say, you should shoot another arrow in the same direction and see where it goes.

There's a bonfire on the site; the workers are getting rid of trash. I think of the man who was the brother of the man who invented paper. His own paper was so coarse nobody would buy it. So he pretended his wife got sick and died; she hid in the cellar. He set his paper on fire. His wife popped out: "Good news, everyone! I've come back to life! My husband's paper is the official currency of the afterlife. I used it to bribe the bureaucrats in hell!" Which is where the tradition of burning fake money in honor of your ancestors comes from. Or so they say.

Put it this way: I'm married to my skyscraper. No guarantee as to how the marriage will work out, but no regrets.

Lan and I love our son (he looks just like me), but that wasn't enough to keep the marriage going. Our horoscopes were incompatible (I'm a Rat and she's a Horse), not that I believe in horoscopes. When we became engaged I gave her an aquarium stocked with the rarest, most beautiful tropical fish, and as a divorce present she got an electric goldfish that swims forever around its bowl. She and our son live in Ningbo. I see him a few times a year. My site manager is from Xishuangbanna, near the Lao border. He belongs to an ethnic minority, and as a young man he wore steel plugs that stretched his lobes. He had an operation to make his ears look normal. But he's still got phantom lobes, extending below his real ones; they itch in hot weather, and he has no way to scratch them.

I press the ▶▶ button on my life—down the scaffolding—down the elevator—and back through the gate and along the street and into the BMW, and reverse out of the spot. And while the car is squawking, the whole city is reversing through the decades . . . to retell its story starting from an era before I was born.

I'm off to see Mama.

I keep her in sheltered accommodation in Daxing, at the edge of the city, beyond the Sixth Ring Road. It's a nowhere zone, between a watermelon field and a motocross park, but it's not as if she ever goes outdoors anyway. I'm as good a son as anybody can expect. I don't personally live with her and cook for her and clean up her messes. I pay other people to do that. I visit her every week.

From the outside, her apartment building looks like any other . . . I walk up one flight . . . I turn the key in the lock . . .

Her home is all golden within. Russian icons. A life-size crucifix. Mama, as usual, is at her computer.

"It's me," I say.

"Can't you see I'm busy?"

"I want to ask you for advice, Mama."

Among the icons, there's a shrine to Dad. He died before

I was born, so I just have to take her word that he was the perfect man, a genius and a devoted husband, somebody I can never hope to be half as good as. Incense sticks and a mango flank a frame holding three photos of him. A wedding photo, on the left; he's wearing a stiff suit borrowed from his work unit. On the right he's a grad student clutching a rock hammer; he and his colleagues, guarded by soldiers, look like prisoners. In the central photo he, along with a dozen other geologists, are performing a loyalty salute. In fact, when they made the picture, Dad was dead already so they cut and pasted him in from another photo. Dad's left fist is raised; his feet are hovering just above the ground, as if he's an Immortal.

I don't know if she believes in any of this stuff deep down: Jesus and Dad and Mao. She doesn't have much faith in me.

A lump of stone Dad dug up in Qinghai is in front of the photos. It's glassy, fused by tremendous heat and pressure. Looking at it is looking into a bottomless pit.

"Help me, Mama."

She's got cataracts so her world is a blur. The text on the screen is bright and expanded—just a few words at a time—and it's all in Russian. She spends her time on foreign literature sites. According to her online profile, she's eighteen and she lives in Moscow and her name is Olga.

"Mama," I say, "Is the real estate bubble going to burst?"

"I'm writing Chekhov fan fiction."

"So tell me, Mama. Should I throw good money after bad?"

"Every story ends the same way. People realize their life is pointless."

"So you're saying I should pull out of the deal?"

"I try to write a happy ending, but it never works."

"So I might as well go deeper into debt, then? That's your advice?"

"You take after your dad. Nothing but a magic voice, that's all you're good for."

I get back in the BMW and I zoom up the Jingkai highway at twenty over the limit. I don't know what to do next. I'm all jangled. It seems like I lose, whichever way I play it. But maybe I win *and* lose. . . . Maybe my competitors—even the people who hate me—won't let me lose. Because if a prime development goes belly-up the whole real estate sector suffers. Beijing's not an imaginary city so long as we all believe in it. It's like with Emperor Qin Shihuang, he built the Great Wall, and hid all those terra-cotta warriors for archeologists to find. Then he died and his courtiers were afraid his empire would collapse if people knew. They parked wagons filled with rotten fish around him, so the stink of his dead body wouldn't be noticed among the general stink.

I learned that story from television, a miniseries about a time traveler poking his nose into bygone dynasties. That was before the government banned the time travel meme;

turning over the past can get you into trouble. The banker who funded me initially (his name's Qin; my building's named after him), an ambitious civil servant is trying to nail him on corruption charges. Qin is punching back; his associates in the media planted a story saying the civil servant and her boss were having an affair and were corrupt themselves. But she retaliated using top-level connections. Now that civil servant, Yang Meixin, she's going after me as well. On her own she isn't powerful enough to harm me—not unless she gets promoted, and I can find a way to stop that. I'll neutralize her boss, Ximen, and I'll save both Qin and myself. Money talks. I just have to make sure Ximen accepts a gift from me as soon as possible, before Yang's promotion goes through. Qin and I are mutually dependent; we often feel like killing each other, but they say that's a sign of a thriving business relationship.

I fact-check online. Emperor Qin wasn't of royal blood at all, according to Records of the Grand Historian. His father was a merchant and his mother was a dancing girl. But he managed to convince everybody he was the rightful ruler, and that's what counts.

So should I? Yes or No?

Right now I need what any man needs. My route takes me near Workers Stadium, where I get stuck in traffic. Guo'an is playing a home game. Thousands of soccer fans dressed in green are blowing green vuvuzelas, and vendors are selling green heart-shaped balloons. (What will happen to the unsold balloons? The vendors will let them go, and up the spare hearts all float into the night.) Me too, I support Guo'an, because you've got to love one team and hate all the others, though it's years since I've made it to a match. *The golden cat is dribbling the ball—I tackle him—I fall on the grass, clutching my shin, faking it, the way professionals do. "The cat fouled me, Referee! He fouled me! I'm entitled to a penalty shot!"* I flash my lights rhythmically and lean on the horn.

The crowd parts, and I make it through to my regular place in Sanlitun.

The madam greets me, "It's you again," like somebody's mother. "What took you so long?" She punches my card: do it ten times, get one free. I check the monitors and I choose a girl I've never had before. Not the prettiest, but she's what I'm in the mood for. "Number forty-four," I say, "My lucky number for today!" Four is the number of death, but four and four make eight, which is the number of prosperity; not that I believe in lucky numbers.

The madam is all smiles to the next customer—"We are honored to welcome you, Detective Zhao!"—who is given a free session with the girl of his choice.

The sweeper, a young man with hair sticking out like a bedraggled crow, limps into the shadows.

I ascend the red-carpeted stairway, the painted ceiling is

a star-filled heaven where the lovers Herd Boy and Weaver Girl are drawn by dragon chariot across a bridge of magpies, and I go through to my assigned room. The rooms are named after provinces of China; mine is Tibet.

Number Forty-Four is here already, on the sofa. She's wearing a golden qipao split up to the thigh. "Hello, darling," she murmurs. "You're *adorable*."

She has an accent I can't place, exotic. Her earrings— turquoise on silver—must be traditional among some ethnic group. "Where are you from, Forty-Four?" I say. "Tibet? Mongolia? Qinghai?"

"I'm from wherever you like," she says.

"Where are you really from?"

The better to consider her answer, she pats a cushion, making room for me. "Do you want me to give you a face reading? Or do you want to skip the intro and I'll give you the most pleasure you ever had in your entire life?"

"First say what you see in me."

She pinches my ear lobe, "You've got auspicious ears." She slides her index finger down the groove between mouth and nose, "You're built for love." And taps my forehead, "Your eyebrows reveal you are destined to hold on to money."

Professional blarney. All the same, she intrigues me. I joke, "You're the first person since my mother to tell me I've got a pretty face."

"It's interesting how many clients talk about their mothers."

She picks up a newspaper, *The Real China Times*, juicy scandals and patriotic editorials, and fans herself coquettishly. I notice an article about my project! I take the newspaper from her, and her hand keeps flapping. The article is complimentary and it ought to be; I paid enough for it.

There's a tattoo on her wrist. "Hey, you've got a qilin there! You're a lucky girl."

"Maybe I can bring you luck?" She raises her hand to her brow, as if saluting. The qilin swivels its horn at me.

I'm reflected in her eyes. "What's your advice, Miss Luck? Should I cut my losses, or should I take out a loan that maybe I can't pay back?"

Of all things, she laughs. "A big man like you, of course you should have a big loan!" To my surprise she's speaking Beijing dialect now and her pitch has dropped too. "I like a man who's not afraid to stake everything."

She's right! That's the kind of man I've got to be. "And I like a girl who's not afraid to stake everything, too, Miss Beijing."

She winks.

Maybe I'm doomed, maybe the whole world is, but that's what gambling is all about. "Let's celebrate! French champagne, for both of us!"

She double-clicks on her tablet. The champagne arrives in the dumb-waiter. She opens it—a controlled explosion.

She switches back to a cooing Mandarin with wrong

tones, "Or do you want me to be from far away?" She poses with fingers parted, one on either side of her mouth, making her lips into a kissy shape.

"No, it's all right," I say. "I could go for a local girl, a beauty from the hutong. What name do you go by, Miss Beijing?"

"They call me Big Eyes."

I'm not going to tell her my real name. "My childhood nickname was Phonograph. My mother said I was a noisy baby."

"There you go again, Phonograph, talking about your mother."

"Were you ever in a tricky situation, Big Eyes? Let's say you did something that wasn't exactly by the letter of the law, and an official threatened to bring you down. How would you defend yourself?"

"You use whatever you've got. Me, I've got my—" pushing forward her bosom and swaying her hips, wafting osmanthus perfume. "And you, you've got your big, big wallet."

She seems resourceful, as well as lucky. Maybe I can find a role for her in my enterprise. "You're good with accents, Big Eyes. Can you do a Shanghai accent?"

"Of course I can do a Shanghai accent," she says in a Shanghai accent, with mutated consonants and glottal stops. "I can do any accent. Somebody called me a little parrot."

"Mm, I happen to know a man who's susceptible to pretty girls from Shanghai. If I asked you to meet him next Friday at eleven a.m. precisely, and give him something from me, do you think you could do that?"

"I could do that."

"His name's Ximen. He'll be in the Octagon Room at a conference center near Ritan Park. I'll give you the address." I take out my pen and write the address on her arm, next to the qilin. "Just wear a business suit and walk in like you belong. You can't miss him; he has a mustache like a villain in Beijing Opera. Message me the second you've done your job." I could give him the bribe personally, but there are spies everywhere; better it goes through an intermediary. He's not going to turn down a gift from a sexy girl, especially one who looks like a younger version of his mistress, and sounds like her too. Once Ximen has taken the bait, I'll go ahead with the Russian deal. "There's a big reward coming your way if you do what I tell you, but if you don't . . ." I thump my chest. "Understood?"

Big Eyes looks scared for a moment, out of her depth. Then she says, "I'm a brave girl!" and she gestures with her sleeve, like a heroine in the Opera.

We clink glasses. "Ganbei!"

For this night anyway, there's just the two of us.

There's a pattern to these encounters. "Karaoke, next," I tell her, "whether you're musical or not!"

She operates the remote, to turn on the equipment. I choose a romantic pop song, a Golden Oldie from the

Deng Xiaoping era. In high school it was the favorite of the girls I was too shy to speak to.

"The old songs are the best," she says.

As if she actually cares for me, she holds my hand.

The screen shows a beautiful landscape: snowy mountains and a lake and a herd of antelope . . . dissolving into a soft-focused man and woman dancing on a cloud . . . while the ball bounces on the lyrics, and she sings the female part, and I sing the male part, and we sing the chorus together, and now there is nothing but instrumental music, telling of love and loss and yearning, and that true love can never die.

THE AVERAGE PERSON IN CHINA

Almost everyone is here already. Professor Zhuang himself was seen getting out of a taxi! The new arrivals jostle beneath the welcome arch, an inflated vinyl structure that quivers as if sharing the excitement; from it hangs a banner: *All-China Conference of Medical Statisticians.* "Come along, come along!" says a person with a red armband. Within the building, in the high, bright atrium, the conferees go through the registration procedure and are ushered farther in toward a rank of elevators. Everybody talks on top of everybody else; the chatter becomes a roar. "Come along, ladies and gentlemen!" says the armband person, almost screaming now, "The plenary session is about to commence!"

It would be impossible to get to know all the conferees, so let's pick the median one: perhaps that man over there, Luo Boqin, twenty-four years and seven months, who is employed in the municipal administration of a small city in Hebei province. From his unhurried gait and the way he hugs his welcome package we may gather he is content enough—and why shouldn't he be? He has a secure job, an "iron rice bowl" as his father calls it. He has a girlfriend, Sufen, a kindergarten teacher. And here he is in Beijing! He's visited the capital before (his home is only a few hours away), but it's quite one thing to be a tourist marveling at Tiananmen or the pandas in the zoo, quite another to be here on serious, adult business. The PA system squeals and commands; the conferees, Luo included, file into the auditorium—and we lose track of him.

When we catch up with him again, it is five p.m. and today's session is over. There will be a reception later in the evening, but now the conferees are heading out, to go back to their hotels and freshen up. He is accompanied by two other men, Zheng Yuan from Shandong province, and Peng Dai from Henan province. The three have been assigned a shared room. Zheng is tall and Peng short, so it is natural that Luo should stand in the middle. Peng estimates the percentage of females at the conference (25± 5%) and Zheng, who is a Party member, has things to explain. "This center wasn't built for the likes of us," he says. "We're here because they don't know where else to put us. But it was intended for high-ranking cadres."

"How do you know?" says Luo.

"I know," says Zheng. "Look at the padded seats in the lecture hall. Look at the stalls in the men's room . . ."

The shuttle bus for their hotel opens its doors at last. Everyone shoves forward. Zheng and Peng make it onboard, but Luo is left behind. He consults his smartphone; it would be almost as quick to walk instead. "Race you to the finish!" Peng mouths at him through a window.

Luo strolls through Ritan Park. Butterflies flicker in his peripheral vision. He texts Sufen: *I'm in Bei* . . . and the character-predictor suggests the *jing*. Not telepathy but statistics: many people are informing other people they're in the capital. *Love you,* he adds. Today is Friday, and the conference ends on Sunday. He feels nostalgia in advance, imagining himself back home, reminiscing about his adventures in the big city. Not that he expects so much. He is aware he is the kind of person who never appears in TV dramas or reality shows, only in audience statistics. He takes a certain pride in being average. He is the bubble in the spirit level, the typical citizen the government should be trying to help. He ambles between camellia bushes, taking a shortcut to the gate.

He arrives at the hotel room. There is a pair of twin beds, also a folding bed, child-size. Peng says to him, "You can curl up, can't you?" while Zheng recites, "From each according to his ability, to each according to his need." Luo's phone rings and it's Sufen prattling about today's happenings at the kindergarten (the children did gymnastics, then they practiced Loving the Flag). It's too much trouble to argue about beds. There is a sink with a mirror above it, and he squints at his reflection. He's growing a mustache; his girlfriend says it makes him look like Sun Yat-sen. He massages his eye muscles to stay awake, just as Sufen instructs her kindergartners. It is night already.

A bus takes the men to their next destination in the dark glittering city.

*

How odd to wake, and feel one's back aching and one's chilly feet sticking out over the foot of the bed, and think *Where am I?* and realize one is in Beijing! Everyone scrambles to get dressed and to the breakfast buffet, and this time the bus drops them on the road outside the conference center, for the forecourt is cluttered with chauffeur-driven Audis. Their own little wobbly arch is overshadowed by a far larger and more rigid arch which proclaims WELCOME THE STEERING COMMITTEE ON FINANCIAL PLANNING AND DISCIPLINE. Inside the atrium, the table with information on medical statistics has been shunted next to the toilets, while the reception area is occupied by men in expensive suits who are being greeted by attractive female staffers and presented with leatherette folders. The men might be senior cadres or bankers or even politicians. Whereas Luo's name is felt-tipped on a paper sticker attached to his lapel, the financial planners wear laminates inserted into lanyards that suspend from their necks; they keep peering at each other's laminates, as if they had cleavage. Their tailored suits cling to their bodies like fur. They grin as they clasp hands. Although there are fewer financial planners than medical statisticians, the former take up more space and they maneuver as they talk. Luo thinks of how an army during peacetime must engage in exercises to remind itself of its function. He is a common soldier and they are the officers. He overhears scraps of their conversation ". . . A firm grip on inflationary tendencies . . ." ". . . Overheating in the real estate sector . . ." ". . . A tolerable level of corruption . . ." When the elevators arrive, the financial planners march on first. The statisticians stare at the blinking lights showing the elevators going all the way to the top and coming down again, to pick them up too.

At the next presentation an epidemiologist asks: "When an outcome is so rare that it happens just once, what does probability theory have to say about it?" The more dutiful copy the question into their notebooks. A napping woman lays her head on her arms as if weeping.

During the recess the statisticians mill in the basement dining area. There is a table with bowls of noodles, to sustain them.

The noodles make Luo thirsty, and he goes in search of water. He can't find a fountain in the basement, so he gets on an elevator and jumps off at a random floor. On this level the carpeting is deep and soft; he can scarcely hear himself walk. And there, around the corner, a water fountain. A financial planner is in front of it, his red silk tie lolling like a dog's tongue; he can't get the hang of the machine. Luo says, "Let me show you." He takes what might appear to be a plain white envelope, and unfolds it till it becomes a cup, and holds it under the spigot. He waves his free hand in front of the photoelectric detector, causing water to gush forth. "Here, this is for you." The financial planner drinks, and drinks again, and throws the crumpled envelope in the trash and struts away without saying a word. Luo realizes his mistake. He made the other man lose face. Yet what else could he have done? At last Luo gets to quench his own thirst, and in the process the sticky label with his name on it detaches itself from his clothing.

How he becomes lost is unclear. The fact is he finds himself walking down a long windowless corridor; the floor underfoot changes from carpet to tiling, and he knows himself to be backstage. There is an office where uniformed women sit with heads bowed over computers; a cleaning closet with a rack of upside-down brooms, their red plastic heads flaring upward; a room containing many monitors showing live images from the security cameras—from the atrium, from the elevators, from various meeting rooms and auditoriums (he recognizes Professor Zhuang; he recognizes the napping statistician, who is now as awake as anybody; in an elevator a man and a woman are kissing). . . . The tiling transmutes into carpeting once again. He passes a small octagonal room with a veneered table, likewise octagonal. There must have been a meeting here recently; a tea tray rests on the table. He thinks to check his phone; the battery is fading. His father left a message: somebody's been trying to reach him, and he should call back. He dashes into the room, pulls a folder from the trash can, and on a random page manages to scribble the number before his phone dies.

The folder contains the program for the Steering Committee on Financial Planning and Discipline. A series of gatherings from morning to evening, followed by a banquet. There is a cup filled with tea on the table, and he drinks from it unthinkingly. He is aware somebody else is in the room and realizing the tea isn't his puts the cup down with a clatter.

A woman in a dark business suit is in the far corner. She is about his own age, pale-skinned, with eyes that make him think of a nocturnal mammal. She shrinks back. It seems she is afraid of him, or of something.

"Hello," he says, nudging the tray aside, as if originally he touched the tea things only in order to clear space.

"Sorry I'm late," she whispers at last. She has a Shanghai accent.

"Can I help you?" he says.

"Ah, I tried to get here by eleven, Mr. Ximen, but . . ."

It's eleven-thirty," he says, glancing at his phone. "And actually I'm not—"

"I hope I'm not interrupting you, Mr. Ximen."

"Not at all." He turns the pages of the program, as if he were busy consulting it. "Actually my name is—"

Her lips quiver. He can smell her osmanthus perfume. She skims over to him in quick little swaying steps. Tears are glowing in her large eyes. "Please, please, Mr. Ximen! Whatever you do, don't promote Yang!"

Her blazing passion makes everything around her, including himself, seem by contrast dim. "No, but ..." he stammers.

She approaches—the cloud of her perfume enveloping him—and stretches forth an arm. He feels her electric touch. Something is transferred from her hand to his. . . . Before he can say a word she retreats, and with one final sob she vanishes from the room.

It is as if he dreamed her. But in his hand is a red envelope. Which he opens. Behold a stash of hundred-yuan bills—more money than he has ever seen in his life.

He cannot move. The fact of the money—the substance and the glory—petrifies him. He has the sensation he is tasting the money: the money is crammed in his mouth, pressed against his teeth, making his gums itch.

He shudders.

He forces himself to think realistically. This is just money, just tinted, engraved paper.

He holds the envelope against his chest. It is not the normal red cash-envelope you might give somebody for Spring Festival. It is hefty, dense; it could almost contain the manuscript for a novel.

He strides to the door. He looks both ways. She's out of sight, whoever she was.

It was a mistake, obviously. It was all a mistake. He should return the gift, shouldn't he? But he doesn't know so much as her name. Might she ask for it back? Unlikely she could identify him; she never looked him in the eye. And that Mr. Ximen—what if he shows up and demands his due? But the payment was surely illegal; Luo has no duty to hand it over; quite the contrary.

He sits down and pours himself more tea. So what's the real story? Likely as not the woman and Yang are rival candidates for promotion. Yang harassed her; once promoted he'd become her boss and she'd be unable to resist his crude advances. If so, a result of Mr. Ximen failing to receive the bribe could be that Yang does get promoted, and so the poor woman will suffer. But really Luo has no way of knowing who's in the right. It might be that Yang is an excellent man who fully deserves promotion, and the woman is a malevolent schemer.

He analyzes his own thoughts, asking himself why he's thinking so rationally (to be sure, this is the kind of person he is, or would wish to be). He must be in a state of shock, he diagnoses; the receipt of a bribe is comparable to being stabbed or shot. His heart beats fast; the red envelope throbs in his pocket. And he's not supposed to be here. He should be attending "Uniformitization of Database Software for Medium-Sized Hospitals: A Step-by-Step Approach."

He goes to the men's room and locks himself in a stall. He counts and re-counts the money. He holds bills up to the light, checking the Mao's face watermark. He pulls the flush, just in case a janitor is wondering what's going on.

He leans against the door frame. He pants and he wipes his forehead with his sleeve, and he feels like sobbing himself.

He returns the way he came, or tries to. A long corridor. He hears his own footsteps—hushed on carpeting, loud on tiles, then hushed again. He sees into an office; the secretaries are wearing party hats and there are balloons tied to the computers. He sees a blue-flowered weed growing from a crack between pane and sill.

An elevator arrives and financial planners make room for him. "We have to question the effectiveness of money supply limitations on restraining inflation in the real estate sector," a short man with a Guangdong accent says. A fat man with glasses says, "But in view of the global situation …" Luo pipes up, "You know, housing prices may have gone up a lot in big cities, like Beijing or Shanghai, but in smaller cities like the one I come from in Hebei, we haven't seen such big changes." The financial planners seem interested in his comment. "Well that's good news for a change," says a man in a shiny suit. "Is that so?" says a man with a hearing aid.

Soon, down in the atrium, he is filled with a quiet joy. Over there, in the corner, some statisticians are chattering away; he smiles at them. He is connected to their world, but also now to the world of money. He feels wise. Rather as when in middle school he first learned about sex he looked at every married person and thought, *He's done that with her. She's done that with him*—so now looking at every financial planner he thinks, *He gives bribes. He takes bribes.* Granted there are exceptions—honest, principled bankers and politicians—just as there are some adults who don't have sex. Luo notices a cleaner operating a floor-polishing machine, and he comprehends even a life like hers more profoundly; he has peeked at the hidden mechanism that makes China tick. If only we truly understood money, there is nothing we would not understand.

He flexes his right hand; it tingles and feels a little numb, as if when the envelope touched his palm a bolt of lightning sparked into him. The unintended gift is a secret he must not reveal, but at the same time he feels a queer yearning to declare it to everybody. He could make up a song about it! He could dance around the atrium, singing about the red envelope!

He decides to go for a walk. (He's missed half this session already; might as well play hooky for the rest.) The glass doors slide apart at his approach, doubling his reflection. Outside, the inflated arch welcoming the statisticians is stable, smaller but proud before the grand arch of the steering committee.

The smog is hazier now; the sun is tofu-colored. Power lines for trolley buses geometricize the sky. There is a store whose signs are in Russian and the customers all seem

Russian too—as if the store fell asleep in Moscow and woke up here. Across the road is the Friendship Store; his father was here in the 1980s. Back then the goods it sold, such as French perfume and Japanese electronics, were unobtainable elsewhere. Only foreigners had access, as well as an elite caste of Chinese. He pictures his father then (younger then than he himself is now), his nose pressed to the window, trying to catch a glimpse of the fabulous products. Now the place is dusty, behind the times. You can get anything in Beijing.

He coughs. Could he one day live in the capital himself? The money in the envelope, colossal though it is by his standards, would not last long here. But the bribe gives him hope. There's so much wealth here, floating around, passing from person to person, in regular and irregular ways . . .

I've got something important to tell you. . . . He will confess his secret to Sufen; her eyes will widen, her jaw will drop. . . . He thinks of her while ogling sophisticated Beijingers. A girl in scarlet silk and a futuristic respirator. A man wearing blue glasses so the pollution is invisible to him. He's been with Sufen a year now. They've not gone all the way; he's never done it with a decent girl. About time, he thinks. Either that, or move on. With his newfound wealth, he could upgrade . . . . *I've got something important to tell you* . . .

A panda glides by on an electric bicycle; person in a panda suit, whatever. Visiting Beijing is like going into the future, he realizes. A while ago one person did this; somebody else copied; a third person is copying that . . . it's like analyzing the progress of an epidemic. In a year or two, all across China, all across the world, we'll see biking pandas.

He returns to the conference center and slips into the back of an auditorium. On the screen a set of equations is projected . . . Markov chains . . . Monte Carlo simulations . . . Zheng is up front, his elbows out as he covers a pad with writing. Peng borrows a pencil sharpener from the woman next to him. The presenter illustrates his speech with over-large motions of the hands, as if communicating with the deaf. "The average person in China," he says, and points at nobody in particular, perhaps Luo. The red envelope nuzzles against his chest. . . . How extraordinary to attend what would otherwise be a boring presentation *when you have money*. Money, he realizes, is a psychotropic drug; it transforms all your perceptions. Money doesn't necessarily make life happier; it makes it different.

*

That night Luo is still enchanted. He says something pleasant and meaningless to the person at the hotel reception desk, the way a rich person might. He evokes the woman in the octagonal room (in his memory, her face is rather octagonal) and the off-stage presences of Mr. Ximen, and of Yang (who, on second thought, might be female, and then there'd be a different set of possible explanations as to what the bribe was intended to accomplish). It is hours since the metamorphosis, but it seems he has been living the bribed life for decades. He reflects on who he was before, and he patronizes his former, ignorant self. Bribery gets a bad press—but is it simply a negative? Far from it. Unlike participants in a regular transaction, the briber and the bribee have to trust each other. For all the woman could know, Mr. Ximen might take her envelope and promote Yang anyway, yet she has faith.

He is untroubled by the mild eccentricity of his room-mates. Peng does push-ups in his underwear. Zheng sits on his bed, poring over a share-tip website. "I know what you're thinking. I know, I know. But wasn't Marx funded by Engels who was an industrialist?" It seems to Luo that Peng's exercises and Zheng's speculations are connected; there are flows of energy, of aspiration.

He goes into the corridor to phone his girlfriend in private. He gets her recorded voice, the pitch of it higher than in reality, *Hello, this is Sufen . . .*

Back in the hotel room the lights are off. Holding his arms out like a sleepwalker Luo finds his child-size bed. He can tell from small noises the others are not yet asleep. He lies on his back, eyes open. He has a yearning to reveal his secret, and why not? The conference will soon be over, and he'll never see these men again.

Into the near dark, into the near silence, he speaks. He doesn't seek to convey the wonder of it, the way his life will forever be divided into the eras Before Bribe and After Bribe . . . how could he? Instead he states the facts of the case, succinctly.

There is a brief pause. Then Zheng says, "She must be crazy!" and Peng laughs, "You devil!"

Don't the others get it? To be sure, every day newspapers report scandals involving millions or billions of yuan, and on soap operas paupers are always coming into riches—but this is a *real* story, that happened to Luo Boqin *himself*. If it happened to him, it could happen to them; it could happen to anybody in China!

He wants to retell the story, making the point of it clear. He'd include all the details—everything he remembers and everything he imagines—so that the scene would be brought to life. The tea in the cup. The gleam in the woman's eyes. Her earrings of silver and turquoise shivering like little bells. Her unearthly beauty when she pleaded, as if her skin were a painted scroll draped around an empty form. The solidity of the packed cash—the undeniability of it. The instant he received the envelope he ceased being exactly himself; to some degree he *is* Mr. Ximen. *No*, he declares silently, as he drifts into sleep, *I will not promote Yang.*

But he is hauled back to consciousness because Peng is reminded of a story of his own. It's about an adventure he had while on a study weekend in Zhengzhou. In essence, as best as Luo can follow (for Peng is narrating in a round-about manner, with many digressions and self-conscious remarks about how amazing it all was) the man found himself in a dark room, and an unknown woman, thinking he was somebody else, kissed him. If that's Peng's peak erotic experience, Luo reckons, then he can't have much love in his life. So much for Henan! (Like many inhabitants of Hebei, Luo looks down on those from the neighboring province.) Besides, the narrative could perfectly well be concluded in one minute, whereas Peng goes on and on, expanding his account, putting in description and dialogue, psychology and philosophy . . . he could be up telling it all night! Hmm, the kiss story sounds suspiciously familiar. (Did Luo read it in a book? Did he come across it online?) But that's not to say it didn't happen to Peng. A story can happen in fiction and in fact too; it can happen to many people in many places, over and over again. Accompanying Peng's yarn, Luo hears snoring, which must be coming from Zheng. The narration and the snoring . . . Peng's droning syllables and the breath forced through Zheng's nostrils. . . . The kiss and the dream. . . . The vastness and the no-size of it all. . . . And eventually, while the story is still being told, Luo nods off.

*

He is up early. He checks out. (The conferees won't be leaving till later, but they have to take their luggage downstairs now.) He fills out an evaluation form. What does he think of the condition of his room: is it GOOD or AVERAGE or POOR? He knows he has to put a checkmark in the first box. The rule—unfair as it may be—is that AVERAGE is unacceptable. If too many guests check AVERAGE then the chambermaid will be fired.

He saunters through the sunny park. Under a hornbeam a white-haired man and woman are belting out a song from a revolutionary opera. The generality about parks is that the old arrive first, then as the day progresses younger people show up. If you looked at a composite image of the typical park user, you'd see an ancient figure becoming more and more youthful as time goes by.

He nears the conference center. The arch of the financial planners has been taken down; the medical statisticians' grooves to the traffic's beat. Outside a restaurant a mother and father stand back to back alongside their infant on a highchair; the family together resembles the characters in the word *Beijing* 北京. He blinks, as if mentally photographing the scene. Then to clear his vision he shakes his head from side to side, letting it all blur—for he has the statistician's faith that to truly understand people it is not enough to know them as individuals, you must know them en masse. On a stretch of sidewalk between a bank and a public toilet

[179]

a water calligrapher is at work: he manipulates his stick, creating wet sentences on the ground. A pair of well-shined shoes drops a coin in the calligrapher's blue cap, and walks on. In this weather the characters evaporate fast. The water calligrapher does not glance up as he dunks the tip in the bucket and writes the quotation: TO SEE THE EMPEROR I'LL CARRY NOTHING BUT TWO SLEEVES OF CLEAR WIND.

Luo foresees that one day he'll be as old as the calligrapher, looking back on his life. After the conference is over he'll go back to his city; he'll treat himself to snappy clothing, rare food, and liquor; a car; he'll find himself a pretty girl or two. . . . The bribe money will run out, but there's more where that came from. Even in medical statistics somebody must want something badly and be willing to pay under the table for it.

Then he thinks of the other life: the one he would have had if he hadn't set out in search of water, and become lost. . . . He'd never be rich; he'd always have money worries. An ordinary life.

Let the old man have a tip. Luo opens his wallet, but he has nothing small on him. He reaches for the red envelope in his pocket and tries to draw out a hundred yuan—as much as the water calligrapher might normally make in a week or a month. But the money is packed close together, and a single bill won't come out.

In both hands he grips the red envelope with all its

contents. He bows. He drops the thing into the water calligrapher's cap. Then as if fleeing the scene of a crime he runs
as fast as he can past office workers eating lunch, past a toilet
paper seller on his tricycle, dashes across the boulevard just
as the lights are turning against him (a BMW screeches and
swerves), and arrives at the conference center more or less
at the same time as the mass of other trudging statisticians.

He feels so lightweight he could lift off and float into the
sky, and survey the capital and all those who are present in
it . . . with a twitch of his fingers he'd return to ground level.
How delightful to visit Beijing! How pleasant to attend this
interesting and informative conference! What a treat to be in
the so-ugly-it's-beautiful metropolis when you know you're
soon to go home! Sufen will be waiting for him at the railroad station. He'll go down on his knees and propose to her,
there and then. No need for a long engagement. They'll have
a "naked marriage"—without owning an apartment, with
little in the way of material goods—as plenty of people they
know are doing these days. When they've saved up enough,
they'll have a child. What more does anybody need?

Where is she right now? At her home? On the bus? No,
she's in the kindergarten! Around her and around her the
little ones dance! She sings the song and they join in the
refrain! He feels she's next to him—that she's in downtown
Beijing and that he's in the kindergarten—the two locations
elide and overlap. The honking taxis and the dancing infants;

the skyscrapers and the array of finger-paintings pinned up on the board. He can't wait even a few hours. He texts, *Will you marry me, Little Cat?* and she texts back, *I'll marry you, Little Dog.*

He should hurry into the building. He mustn't be late for Professor Zhuang.

He notices one more text. It's from that number that called earlier, asking him to call back. It turns out to be from Human Resources. *We are pleased to inform you that you have been awarded a bonus for satisfactory work of 300 yuan.* When one thing goes right, everything goes right! On the strength of the bonus, he'll take his fiancée out for a meal and buy her a drink. Then, for the first time, they'll rent a room at a love hotel . . .

Luo Boqin passes through the sliding glass doorway, and he fades from view, and we never see him again. But we can be fairly confident that he will remain close to the national median. He and his wife and their child will be an average family, with an average standard of living, making their home in an average city. Let them stand for all the others we never get to know. If the Luo's are going through hard times, then China is going through hard times. If the Luo's are doing well, then China is doing well.

THE WATER CALLIGRAPHER'S
WOMEN

She says it was a man, an old man (but all men are old to her), which man, what did he look like, what was he wearing, what did he do

a man with a stick, a long stick, what was it, a hard stick, yes, the man's stick was long and hard, yes, a man with a long stick and it was wet at the end

ai! it must be

Water Calligrapher, Water Calligrapher Wu, he has a stick, a broomstick, and he ties a red nylon sponge to the end, he carries a pail of water, he dips the sponge in the water, and he calligraphs characters on the ground

he has a cap too, a blue peaked cap like people used to wear in the old days, and he places it on the ground with the inside showing, and sometimes people drop money in it, if they like his calligraphy

he used to do his calligraphy in the waste ground next to the supermarket, but the supermarket expanded and took over the waste ground, so he moved to the marble terrace in front of the stock trading office, but they demolished the stock trading office, marble terrace and all, so he moved to opposite the post office, but the Urban Security officials shooed him away, so now he does his calligraphy on the dusty pavement behind the public toilet

and not many passersby come down there (it's a dead-end alley, nobody walks by on the way to somewhere else) and he can't make much money, but at least he's left alone

he's an expert calligrapher, nobody said he wasn't, he loads his sponge with just enough water but not too much, his sponge-strokes have style, he handles the long stick like an ink brush, like he might be a famous artist sketching a landscape with figures, he knows how to twist the sponge as he slides it along so as to "hide the tip," if you stood a way off and squinted, you'd think the stick was a brush and his whole body is a hand

he calligraphs

phrases, important phrases, he likes phrases that have four characters apiece, because they fit onto his four rectangular paving slabs, but he can do more, oh yes, eight characters, sixteen, there's no limit to how many characters he can calligraph, one after the other, if he puts his back into it

tell us some of the things he's calligraphed

quotes from politicians and poets and philosophers, SUFFERING MAKES NATION NOBLE and PALEST INK, BEST MEMORY, and enterprising Baker Hurong commissioned Calligrapher Wu to write a slogan: EAT DELICIOUS

FRENCH-STYLE PASTRIES, somebody comes out of the toilet, and they're inspired to eat a foreign pastry (are the pastries good, has anybody eaten Baker Hurong's French-style pastries, yes they are very good, you should try one)

what else has he calligraphed

EXPERIENCE COMB BALD MAN and PAPER CANNOT WRAP FIRE and IF BOW, BOW LOW

when is Calligrapher Wu at work

he's at work in spring and summer and autumn, he can't work in the rain, of course, when there's too much rain his own water is invisible, we've seen him in the mist, we've even seen him in drizzle, a drop here and a drop there he can cope with, but a proper downpour, ah, he has to wait for it to come to an end and the ground to dry up, and in winter, once the snow comes, of course he can't work at all (where does he go in winter, how does he survive)

is Calligrapher Wu an outsider, a migrant from the provinces, no he's not, because Urban Security came and checked his ID; he's got an ID and a residence permit, just like you and me, he's a Beijinger born and bred, well, anybody can tell just to look at him, a failure, a loser, a bit funny in the head, we'll grant that, all the same he's one of our own, but we never would have suspected, with Little Jiaojiao of all people, such a sweet girl with a lovely smile, and smart too

what did he say to her, that's a trick question, why is it a trick question, because Calligrapher Wu never speaks, he can't speak, no, he can speak, he can speak as well as anybody, he simply never does, and it's not that his vocal chords don't work or his lungs, because they do, when the bad boys steal money from his begging cap, he curses them out, oh yes he does, but not in words, he howls, he howls like a dog when you kick it, like a cat when you tread on its tail, he shakes his stick at them and he splatters them with his water, but it seems he sees no reason to speak most of the time and maybe he has a point there, all the useless conversation the rest of us have, oh it's windy, my it's windy today, what a lot of wind, yes it is extremely windy, I'm coming, you're going, I'm going, you're coming, yes very windy, I'll say it's windy, extraordinarily windy, I've never known so much wind

but the fact of the matter, there's no denying, Calligrapher Wu and Little Jiaojiao

the police arrested him

and the police released him without charges, which is shocking, because if not him then who, somebody else in the neighborhood, an unknown person, and that's more scary, because with Calligrapher Wu, at least we can warn the children, stay away from him, he's got a long stick, a long hard stick that's wet at the end, he's crazy, he means trouble, but if not him could be anybody, kindly bus driver, school guard who's always ready with a quip, it might even be a woman, a nursery school teacher, or one of those gossipy biddies on the Residents Committee so proud of her red armband, it might be any one of us, it might be me or you

but even if Calligrapher Wu is innocent, how come the police didn't get him to confess

it turns out that Calligrapher Wu's wife pleaded

he has a wife, we didn't know he had a wife, how can a man like him have a wife, where is she, what sort of person is she, what does she do with herself while he's putting water on the paving stones, leaving his mark like a dog

well not exactly his wife, it was his ex-wife rather, well that's just about conceivable, maybe he wasn't always like this, maybe once he was normal, a decent citizen, then a blow to his head, a brain tumor, a work accident, and he becomes the kind of fellow who calligraphs behind the public toilet, and he must have had an education because he's literate, and his calligraphy is excellent, nobody ever said it wasn't, he can make marks with his sponge in eight different ways, he has a fine hand and a fine memory, in the spring he calligraphs a poem about spring, and in the summer about summer, and in the autumn about autumn, and in the winter, ah who knows what happens to him in the winter

don't ruin my life, the ex-wife pleaded with the police, don't ruin the life of our child

a child, the Water Calligrapher has a child, the very idea seems absurd, yet why not, when we think about it, a man with a long hard stick that's wet at the end, and he calligraphs classic poems, he can charm them, with poems like that a man can go a long way, like that poem about boating on the lake with courtesans during the Tang Dynasty, well if that doesn't charm the birds from the trees we don't know what does

something like this, we weren't there ourselves but we can imagine it, the ex-wife went to the mother of the girl, and woman to woman she made her plea, she pressed one hand against the palm of the other and pressed them both against her chest, she bowed, she bowed lower, we wouldn't be surprised if she went down on her knees and kowtowed like in those costume dramas on TV, she cried, yes surely she cried, tears streaming from her eyes, making little patterns on her cheeks and neck, and on the dusty ground

and the mother discussed it with the father, and they spoke to the girl, and the parents spoke to the police, and it was agreed it would be best for everybody if the charges were withdrawn

and there he was back again, brazen, writing his words on the stones, OLDER GINGER, HOTTER SPICE and STEAL BELL, EARS COVERED and MOUTH DAGGER, HEART TOFU.

so we spoke to the street artists, we don't normally speak to them, why would we speak to them, except to say, here's some money, I enjoyed that song, I heard that song before, that song has a ring to it, can you play that song over again, can you play a different song, can you play the song with the crow in it, can you play a love song, can you play a folksong from Qinghai province, if I sing you a song can you sing it back to me only ten thousand times better, thank you, here's some money, my isn't it windy, oh it's so windy, it's extremely windy today, I've got to run or I'll miss my bus, but today we asked about the Water Calligrapher, what's his story, what's going on with him, what happened to him long ago, there's the blind man who plays the erhu, and there's the not-blind man who plays the erhu, there's the juggler, and there's the acrobat, and there's the man who passes solid steel rings through each other, we don't know how he does it, there's a secret to it, and the whole point of secrets is that they're secret, but today the street artists all told us if we want the truth of the matter we should squat on the dusty ground at the end of the alley near the public toilets and we should have a conversation with the Water Calligrapher himself (but how can we speak with a man who doesn't speak)

there once was a man and his wife and their baby daughter, he was a teacher in the high school and she was a teacher in the elementary school, and he and his wife took part in the rallies, they chanted the chants, they danced the Loyalty Dance, they led the others in the chanting and the dancing, they bowed low with their arms tied behind their back, they wore a dunce cap and a placard around their necks saying "I am a Snake Monster and an Ox Demon," they were beaten with a stick, his wife had to denounce him, she had to divorce him and she had to marry his chief accuser, a factory worker, who became the stepfather of their little daughter, and the teacher had to clean toilets, and times changed and the teacher was rehabilitated, he could be a teacher again, but as a teacher he could be sent anywhere in Greater Beijing, he could be sent far from his home, whereas the toilet cleaner cleaned the public toilet right near the home of his wife and daughter, that is, the people who used to be his wife and daughter and who are still his wife and daughter in his head, he saw them every day, and one day when the daughter was old enough, he tried to explain, he tried to tell her that he was her daddy, that he was her real daddy, that he used to be her real daddy, but she loved her daddy, that is the man she called Daddy, and she didn't listen to the strange man with the brush and the mop, and he never tried again, and the toilet cleaner reached retirement age and another toilet cleaner was hired, and the daughter herself married her childhood sweetheart and they all lived in the area where they'd grown up, the familiar scribble of alleys and houses and shops, and the daughter had a daughter, and the daughter's daughter looked like the daughter who looked like her mother, and when the daughter's daughter was old enough the retired toilet cleaner tried to communicate with her in turn, but this little girl didn't understand, she didn't understand the slogans and she didn't understand why we have to denounce the Four Olds and she didn't understand when he did the Loyalty Dance and she didn't understand how a man could be a snake or an ox and she didn't understand his hiss and his bellow, and she didn't understand his confession

I committed crimes against the people

So that the people take me as the object of the dictatorship

I have to lower my head and admit my guilt

I am not allowed to speak or act incorrectly

If I speak or act incorrectly

Beat me and smash me

Beat me and smash me

and she didn't understand when he hit himself across the head with his own stick, and she didn't understand when he hit himself again and again till he was bleeding, and she didn't understand when he cried out calling her by the name of her grandmother, and he tried to give her a red envelope, i.e. and she didn't understand when he hit himself across the head with his own stick, and she didn't understand when he hit himself again and again till he was bleeding, and she didn't understand when he cried out calling her by the name of her grandmother, and he tried to give her a red envelope, and she ran away down the alley, and he came after her down the alley, there was a pussy cat and a butterfly and a rusty bicycle somebody had dumped there, and she needed to go wee-wee, she really, really needed to go wee-wee, but it was late and the man was between her and the public toilet, and the man was coming closer, and the little girl was too scared even to scream as the ruined old man came after her with his long hard stick wet at the end

he assembles his pail of water and his stick and his sponge, he confesses in public, the old man can no longer speak but he can still confess, he calligraphs his confession for all of us on the dry paving stones, and some of us are trying to read over his shoulder, and some are trying to read from the sides, and some are trying to read upside down, what's that stroke, what's that word, what's the vital part we might be missing, what's the beginning of the story and what's the middle of the story and will there ever be an end to it, and before the man's life is even over the wind blows and the sun breaks through, and one after the other all the characters evaporate.

THE SADNESS AND THE BEAUTY OF
THE BILLIONAIRE

– I liked your last book. No, really I did. How much money did you make from it?

– Really?

– Is that all?

– And how much from the residuals?

– Oh.

– Well, you know what they say about making money. The most fun you can have with your clothes on.

– Are you blushing, or is that a skin condition?

– And what was it that the *Times* said about you? "Gets inside the heads of people living in China today." Of course, the *Times* is no expert. The *Times* is talking through its ass. But still, it's always nice to be appreciated.

– I got through you in one sitting. I couldn't put you down.

– A mutual friend suggested you. She said you might be what I'm looking for. And she's right. You are.

– You're a stereotype of a certain kind of Sinophile, and I mean that in a positive sense. Western man goes to China. Western man learns Mandarin. Western man studies Chinese history and literature. Western man has a string of

Chinese girlfriends. . . . And I'm not saying you got China *wrong,* but . . . let's face it, you're limited. Sure you know students and professorial types, and I guess you interviewed peasants and workers and, I don't know, scientists, and you can write about those, but there are other people—people with influence—important people—people with their hand on the wheel—okay, I'll say it, *rich* people—and that's what you should be writing about! And you have no access to those circles.

– Maybe I can help you there.

– To understand China, you have to be above a certain income level. Rich and powerful people talk to other rich and powerful people. They don't tell the truth to you. Unless you have a very special connection.

– Think about it. That's all.

– Do you want any coffee or anything, to keep you going?

– Glenfiddich?

– Your *next* book. Your *eagerly awaited* . . . I can see it's a problem for you. Especially when your first book was, how shall I put it, *critically acclaimed.* You want to write something more successful this time. You're *entitled* to success.

– I'd like to help you. And you can help me.

– You want anything with that? Cream? Sugar?

– Can you reach out with your foot and turn on the air purifier?

– Thank you. I love everything about Beijing apart from

the smog. And I'm not so keen on certain Beijingers either; I think of them as smog people. Beijing puts the OMG in smog!

– That was a joke. Get it? You can steal it and put it in your book. That's what writers do, isn't it? I don't mean *steal,* I mean, *borrow,* I mean, *share.*

– Did you ever think of writing a mystery? The kind of book people read on planes.

– It's good to be back. When you grow up in Beijing, everywhere else seems a village or a museum.

– Oh and by the way, I'm not here. Understood? Officially I'm not anywhere in the country. According to my Twitter feed I'm by the pool at Chateau Marmont, taking a meeting with a bankable star.

– It's late night here, and it must be close to dawn over there. I don't know what time it is in my head.

– My shoes hurt. I'll just slip them off. You don't mind, do you?

– A sip? Go on. There's plenty more in the minibar.

– Cheers! Bottoms up!

– Yes.

– Yes.

– That's a valid point you're making.

– Yes.

– You're just a little uncertain. You want to hear more details, before you commit. That's okay. I like reluctant men.

– You're blushing again. Or is it something you're seeing your dermatologist about?

– You're not too "pure" to care about the bottom line. I'm not saying it's your only motivation. You write to make your mark. You write to impress other writers. You write to get laid. But I know plenty of writers in the industry—Chinese and American both—and when you people get together, practically all you talk about is money.

– Maybe it's different for you fiction writers, but I don't think so.

– "Why me?" Well, I'll give you several reasons why you. Number one: you're not Chinese. Readers don't believe Chinese authors; they think the author was bribed to present things from a certain angle. Number two: you're not a journalist; ditto. Number three: you write in English. We'll do the book in English first, so when we bring out the Chinese version it'll come across as trustworthy. Number four: you've got a literary reputation, and that's worth more than you might think. . . . Number five . . .

– What else do you want me to tell you? That everybody loves you? That you're a cross between Shakespeare and J. K. Rowling? That's not the point. I studied to be a producer at USC, and the one thing they taught me—I knew it before I started—is that if you have enough confidence in yourself, you'll convince other people too. The other thing I got out of it is connections, connections, connections . . .

– But seriously . . . I respect you. You know the old Hollywood joke about the starlet so dumb she slept with the writer? Well, I don't buy that. . . . Your experience, that's exactly what's needed for this project. The biography is going to be true and nothing but the truth, but you're going to use your fictional skills. Nobody literally remembers dialogue that happened years ago, so you're going to imagine it, the way it must have been. You'll make up the "telling details." You'll select the achievements of his life and present them in a way to make the reader sympathize and admire . . . I don't claim to know much about writing. At USC I took The Screenplay as a course requirement. They taught us how to write master scenes. There's a rule: "Begin after the beginning. End before the end." At first the viewers don't quite understand what's happening; just when they begin to catch on, the scene is over. Cut.

– Any writer can churn out a story about a poor, suffering migrant worker and make the reader sympathize with him. But only a really talented writer can make the reader sympathize with a man who has a substantial financial cushion. Think about it. You want to write about the whole spectrum of Chinese society. Daddy included.

– Fiction wasn't his thing. He read Chinese history to relax, the more ancient the dynasty, the more he was eager to learn about it. You wouldn't have guessed that about him, would you? He kept the *Analects* on his nightstand.

– On the surface he was charming, and he could be tough. Most people didn't realize how sensitive he was, deep down.

– Like you. You have your sensitive side.

– It was my assistant, Linlin, who suggested your name. Was she one of your girlfriends too? You're blushing again. I wouldn't have thought she was your type.

– You don't mind my asking, do you? I'm interested in people, and how they're connected to other people. I network. You're like me in that regard, aren't you?

– How do you research your books? What percentage of your interviews do you actually use? How do you transcribe them? An app on your smartphone? Do you take real stories and just change the names?

– I see. You adapt. You alter. You combine. That's precisely the skill set I'm looking for.

– Did you ever get sued?

– No, of course not. Just asking.

– You're a professional. You take a real story and stand it on its head and turn it inside out, and it becomes something completely different. And I admire you for it.

– The air purifier is blowing in my face. Could you turn it the other way?

– Thank you.

– Are you comfortable yourself?

– If it's blowing in your face now, you can move over here. Nearer me.

– He loved me, you know. I sometimes think he loved me more than he loved himself.

– *The story of a man who exemplified modern Chinese business practice . . . The entrepreneur with his finger on the pulse of the soaring dragon . . .* You can improve on that. You're the writer: not me. You show me how good you are.

– He grew up ordinary, you know, in Fengtai District. Not poor, not rich. He began his career in the eighties. He was a private banker in an age when nobody knew if private banking was legal or not. Like Deng Xiaoping said, "It doesn't matter if the cat is black or if the cat is white. What matters is if it can catch mice." He caught a lot of mice.

– When I was a girl, he took me to his childhood home. The neighborhood had been demolished and redeveloped. There wasn't anything to see.

– Well, no need for you to research that part of his life. You don't want to bore the readers, going on about his childhood and his ancestors. Enough to describe him the way he was, at the peak of his success.

– He was a visionary. He saw possibilities. He was always on the cutting edge.

– Not just finance, no.

– He transcended his role. We live in an information age, and he had the genius to realize it. There was a project in Qufu that he personally catalyzed. He enabled a Chinese company to beat foreign competition for the construction contract. A patriot, to the bone. That happened five years ago; it was a high point in his career and he never looked back.

– At his funeral, thousands came to pay their respects: politicians, captains of industry, high-net-worth individuals, and ordinary people too. Even his rivals, even people who opposed him, who tried to bring him down, even they respected him.

– He had certain medical issues. Heart palpitations. Low blood pressure. I don't think that had anything to do with it, actually.

– And the irony is, his business empire was really taking off, just in his last year ... Real estate ... Currency swaps ... Import/export ...

– He was getting involved in the world of film, too, raising capital for a multinational coproduction. I took him to Cannes. Sure, he got involved as a favor to me, but not just as a favor to me. He was genuinely interested. He was a man of wide interests.

– Like all great men, he made enemies.

– The world needs to know what he was like. It's the least I can do for him.

– I don't know much about your kind of writing, but I know how it works in film. Let's say you're an ambitious young screenwriter: you pen a script and you pull all your strings till you find an established screenwriter who's willing to let it appear under his name. A top screenwriter might get the writing credit for a dozen films a year. You keep at it, ghostwriting and building up your credentials, till finally a producer agrees to let you take the writing credit yourself. You're a success. So now young screenwriters are eager to ghostwrite for you. If your name's on it, you didn't write it; if you wrote it, your name isn't on it. That's pretty much the rule in China. Maybe it's a little different in Hollywood.

– What I'm saying is: you don't have to do the whole book yourself. You write the pitch and an outline. I'll find people who are experts in different fields, who'll help you with the rest. You just translate their work into English. You add your metaphors and symbols, that you're so good at. Your special touch of magic.

– Their contributions will be from different points of view and written in various styles, but that's not a problem for you. You'll weave them all together.

– The way I'm thinking, each chapter will focus on some individual who he helped. You've heard of Six Degrees of Separation? Well, in the business world, it's more like two or three degrees. Directly and indirectly, he was involved in projects all across China. People he never even met, they benefited from his actions. A financier *and* humanitarian.

– Let's just stick to people in Beijing. I've nothing against the rest of China. I do half my business in Shanghai. . . . Did you know that in the backlot in Hengdian they constructed a life-size replica of the Forbidden City, accurate in every detail? They even copied the graffiti. But why go there when you can go to the real thing?

– I've got a quote for you. His last foreign engagement was at the World Economic Forum in Switzerland. Professor Schwab introduced him: "You, sir, have founded a thriving business that affects the lives of many people. You are renowned for your eloquence and graciousness. You have one foot in China and the other foot in the broader international business community. Dr. Qin, welcome in Davos!"

– He never went to college, but he had three honorary doctorates from colleges he donated to.

– Everybody wanted a piece of him.

– You always think: Is there anything more I could have done?

– He was under stress, sure. He was drinking, but not, you know, to excess. And taking pills.

– Another Glenfiddich?

– Can you pour me one too?

– Thank you.

– Ganbei!

– You should come to Davos. There are statesmen and billionaires and a few specially selected creative types. There are lectures and workshops, and parties that go on all night. They call it the village that never sleeps. It's like Burning Man—only it's in the snow, instead of the desert, and participants wear suits instead of body paint. . . . You can come to Davos next year, if you like, join my entourage. You can join my camp at Burning Man too. . . . Nobody ever sleeps in either place. Maybe dreams a little.

– Your next book will be a bestseller. How do you feel about that?

– I know it will. I'll buy up enough copies to take it to the top of the chart. And I'll push the English version too.

– The world needs to see the human face of Chinese business. The people you read about in your news feed aren't typical. They're exceptions to the rule. Somewhere in China there's a corrupt politician with an extravagant lifestyle; there's a civil servant who embezzles millions; there's a flagrantly thieving banker; and that's what makes the headlines! But what about all the decent financiers, the ones who—I won't say everything they do is always strictly legal, because the law is not defined in every case—they follow generally accepted standards. They grease the Chinese miracle!

– I'm not putting it very well, but you can. You with your gift for words.

– I'll have Linlin give you the contract.

– Why not?

– If I offered you a million dollars to write one sentence, you'd agree, wouldn't you?

– Now we've established you're a whore, so we're just haggling over the price.

– That was an old joke. I didn't mean it personally.

– You won't just be doing it for me, you'll be doing it for yourself. You're ambitious. You want to write an important book, a necessary book. We're in the Chinese century, and money is what it's all about. China and money—what greater theme could there be?

– You're tempted, I know you are. You're intrigued.

– You'll have total creative control. I'll pay you half up front and half on delivery. A share of the royalties, too. Of course, I'll make the final editorial decision, but you can retain rights to your own version, your "director's cut."

– In films, people are motivated by love, but in real life they're motivated by money.

– Maybe nobody else can write it, but you can. That's what I liked about your last book, the way you got inside the heads of people living in China today. The truth always lies in the gaps between the stories.

– Oops. Sorry.

– The good thing about Glenfiddich is that it hardly leaves a stain.

– Have a Kleenex. Have as many as you want.

– You're welcome.

– If he had one defect, it is that he was *too* caring. He tried to help everyone. In his early days, before he upgraded his operations, he gave individualized financial backing to middle-ranking persons in provincial cities, and not all of them were worthy of his trust.

– It was an opening for his enemies. He was accused of irregularities he had no control over.

– He passed away at the height of his powers. Without any scandal, that could have destroyed his credibility, and mine too. I think if you could ask him, he'd not regret the timing.

– One of the things he taught me: There's a time to invest your stake, and there's a time to cash out.

– I was the last person to see him.

– No.

– No, actually.

– He was visiting me in LA. As a matter of fact he was staying in a suite at the Fairmont.

– Yes.

– No.

– A scotch or two, as a nightcap. Prescription pills to cope with jet lag.

– I went home, and the chambermaid found him in the morning.

– The police found traces of barbiturate in his scotch, so they jumped to the conclusion. . . . He wasn't a quitter. Even if he judged it was strategically necessary, he wouldn't have done it on his own.

– It was an accident. That's what the inquest concluded.

– Let's just agree it was an accident.

– More coffee, or tea, or . . . ? I guess there's food in the minibar, if you really must eat, instant noodles, whatever. Glenfiddich?

– It won't happen again. There are no sleeping pills here, nor any kind of downers. I don't believe in sleep.

– It must be morning already in California. Excuse me while I tweet. I'll say I'm in Malibu, by the ocean, having a power breakfast.

– He always wanted me to find a husband. And I'm not saying there aren't great marriages out there, but in my experience. . . . He wanted a grandchild, really.

– I miss him.

– He had his tender side. Nobody else knew that, but I knew.

– I mixed him the drink, and I put it to his lips, and I held him in my arms, till it was over.

– You'll find a way to put that into our book, won't you, without actually saying it? The sadness and the beauty of the billionaire.

– You remind me of him, in a way. Your ambition. Your yearning. Your desire to reach out.

– It's hot in here.

– I guess blush is your natural color.

– I'm tired, but I'm never tired enough.

– You think you're the opposite of me, but deep inside we're the same.

– Yes.

– Yes.

– Hold me.

– Yes.

– Shut your eyes, and I'll turn the music on.